Follow Andrina Adamo's dancing career through these
new editions of the Drina ballet books.

The Drina books:

Drina Dances in Paris

by
Jean Estoril

SIMON & SCHUSTER
YOUNG BOOKS

Cover artwork by Kevin Jones
Cover design by Terence Kingston
Illustrations by Jenny Sanders

Text copyright © Jean Estoril 1962

First published in Great Britain by Hodder & Stoughton Ltd
Second edition published in Great Britain by MacDonald & Co
(Publishers) Ltd

This edition published in 1992 by
Simon & Schuster Young Books
Campus 400
Maylands Avenue
Hemel Hempstead HP2 7EZ

Printed and bound at Cox & Wyman Ltd, Reading, Berkshire,
England

British Library Cataloguing in Publication Data available

ISBN: 0-7500-1266-8

CONTENTS

BOOK ONE
Ballet at Christmas

1
Home from New York

"Well, Drina, I suppose you're thrilled that we're nearly home?" Mrs Chester asked, eyeing her granddaughter thoughtfully. "On Monday you'll find yourself back at the Dominick."

"Oh, yes, Granny, it'll be wonderful!" But Drina said it absently, her eyes on the blue-grey waters of the Channel and the distant, misty English coast.

Mr and Mrs Chester were lying in deckchairs on the sheltered aft deck, for there were still a few hours of the voyage left. The *Victoria* was expected to reach Southampton by about four o'clock, and that evening would see them home again at their flat in Westminster.

Drina was not fond of sitting in deckchairs; she said that the very sight of people lying in rows made her feel restless. She never did more than pause for a short while to talk to her grandparents and then she was off again, either to walk the deck or else to swim or play games. So now she stood poised in her white sweater and jeans. Mrs Chester hated to see girls wearing trousers of any kind, but Drina had overruled her, as she managed to do over so many things nowadays. In only about two weeks' time she would be fifteen, though it was difficult to believe. She was often annoyed at being taken for little more than twelve, because she was so small and slim.

"Do you mean to say that you won't be glad to get back to your dancing?"

"Oh, yes, I shall be very glad. And I shall have to work and work, because, after all, I've missed nearly a whole month of term."

"You'll soon catch up. Don't go and overwork or you'll undo all the good of the holiday. I must say that you're looking splendidly well. Nearly the middle of October and you're still as brown as a berry."

"It was partly all that wonderful heat in New York," Drina said. "And it's been lovely nearly all the way back. My tan will go very soon, though, once I'm back in London and the weather begins to get wintry."

"I hope it doesn't get wintry too soon. It's been a splendid trip, though I must admit that I found the heat in New York rather too much for me."

Drina wandered away, her straight black hair lifted, once she was out of the sheltered corner, by the boisterous wind. Mrs Chester gazed after her, a frown creasing her brows.

"I just can't make Drina out!"

"Why? What's the matter?" Mr Chester put down his book, removed his spectacles and looked at his wife enquiringly. "I thought I heard you say that she looks splendid."

"So I did and she does. But there's been something about her lately that puzzles me. I noticed it all the time we were in New York."

"She was happy. She adored New York and she was so busy rehearsing for that dancing show with Yolande Mason. It's just that she's growing up."

"I suppose you're right," said Mrs Chester, though without much conviction. She had brought Drina up since she was only eighteen months old. Drina's father had died when she was only a small baby and her mother, the great dancer, Elizabeth Ivory, scarcely nine months afterwards. Mrs Chester thought of Drina as almost her own child, but she had never really understood her, finding in her granddaughter's imaginative character much that she slightly regretted and that she put down, rightly or not, to the fact that Drina's father had been Italian. Drina had always been a slave to only one desire – to be allowed to dance – and she had gone to the Dominick Ballet School nearly three years ago.

Mrs Chester would have been glad to keep her only grandchild out of the ballet world, but that had proved impossible. Now she was resigned to it, but Drina's new mood was, apparently, nothing to do with dancing. It was just that – well, Mrs Chester simply couldn't put it into words. But she had noticed a change nearly a month ago, when they had been sailing to America on the *Queen of the Atlantic*. Drina seemed to have grown older suddenly, more dreamy and thoughtful and more prone to unexpected moods.

"I suppose she'll be herself again when she gets back to all her friends at the Dominick," Mrs Chester added with a faint sigh and, closing her eyes, gave herself up to the last hour or two of total relaxation.

Drina herself mounted the steps to the Games Deck and stood in a sheltered corner, gazing back at the long cream wake of the ship. After a week on board, the *Victoria* seemed very familiar and it would certainly be strange to sleep in her own bed at home that night. She had made a few friends during the voyage, but it had been nothing like that much more wonderful and exciting trip on *Queen of the Atlantic*, with New York ahead and the company of Yolande and Grant Rossiter. Grant ... Drina caught her lower lip between her teeth, thinking of all those crowding and important memories of the voyage out and the time in New York.

New York and Grant ... They were still, even after a week at sea in that odd limbo of sky and water, so very vivid. She still missed both the city and Grant with an intensity that sometimes startled and almost frightened her. When she said goodbye to Grant after that unexpected and wonderful trip up the RCA Building on the last Friday evening she had thought herself calm and resigned. She had fallen in love with him when she met him that first day on the *Queen of the Atlantic*, and it had been sheer luck that Mr and Mrs Rossiter had liked her grandparents and had set themselves to entertain all three of them during their time in New York. So she had seen Grant again and again, and he had seemed to like her, though he must have thought her very young. Grant was, after all, nearly nineteen, but he had not patronised her. He had been almost as friendly as though she had been his own age. He had been wonderful ... The memory of his fair hair and soft drawling voice was still sharp and clear.

But it was partly the knowledge that her memories of him would fade that made Drina feel so sad. Grant had gone; there were now more than three thousand miles of sea between them and, though he had said that he might one day see her again in London, she did not really believe it.

In bed at night in her cabin she had tried to get the thing in perspective. She had fallen in love before she was fifteen, and it had been completely unexpected – something that she had not imagined happening to her for years yet. In fact, she had thought herself entirely dedicated to her dancing, and that was how things *must* be again. Her friends ... the ballet school in Red Lion Square ... endless hard work.

"I *must* forget him," she told herself for the hundredth time, as she stood alone there on the Games Deck. "Even if he wasn't a New Yorker and so far away, it couldn't lead anywhere or do either of us any good. I've got years more at the Dominick. I'm going to be a dancer."

But she was haunted still, as she descended the steps and walked round and round the Promenade Deck, by those memories of New York.

It had been a dream. It must have been a dream! It had seemed so, even when the city was most real. And how beautiful it had been in the autumn sunshine, with the skyscrapers soaring up into the blue sky. And even more beautiful at night, with a million lights. From the top of the RCA Building ... the jewelled bridges, the blaze of Broadway, the Empire State Building jewelled, too, with the beacon light swinging round.

Drina forced her mind back to the Dominick, where she would be again on Monday morning.

The ship docked at five past four and, with very little trouble going through the Customs, the Chesters and Drina were soon sitting in the London train. Then they were speeding across the October countryside, where a faint blue mist wreathed about the golden trees. They seemed to reach London very quickly and there they were at familiar Waterloo and driving away in a taxi towards Westminster.

"So odd to be home!" Drina murmured, as they went up in the lift and her grandfather put his key in the door. There was a pile of letters on the mat and he swept them up and put them on the hall table, to be looked at later. Drina was reminded of her return from Edinburgh – astonishingly only five weeks ago – when there had been a similar pile and amongst them Jenny's letter giving the bad news of the bankruptcy of her father's firm. Jenny ... How *was* Jenny?

She had not long to wait, for half an hour later, when she was in her room unpacking, the telephone bell rang and Jenny was on the line.

"Oh, *Drina*! You're really home? I wasn't sure ... I thought I'd just try. From a call-box."

"Jenny! Oh, it's lovely to hear you!" Jenny was Drina's best friend, even though they met rather seldom. Jenny lived in the Warwickshire town of Willerbury and had lately had to leave her old school and go to Grossdale Comprehensive.

Just to hear Jenny's voice made New York really seem an incredible dream.

"Lovely to hear *you*. Thank you for all your letters and cards. You loved it, then?"

"Oh, Jenny, I did! I didn't want to come home. It – it was far too short."

"What? You wanted to stay there and give up the Dominick – and me?"

"Not *stay*. Not forever. But for longer. I wouldn't give you up if you were twenty thousand miles away. How are you?"

Jenny said in that slightly forced voice that cut Drina to the heart:

"Not so bad. I've been to the farm today. Saturday, you know. I go both Saturday and Sunday. It keeps me sane. I do rather hate all these commercial subjects.

"I wish you didn't have to do them."

"So do I, but I daren't think about it too often. When are you coming to see us? Do come before we move into the smaller house."

"I don't know. I'll ask Granny. Perhaps next week end. I've *got* to see you." Though Drina remembered her last very short visit with embarrassment. It had been dreadful to see the Pilgrims in trouble.

"I'll expect you. Come on Friday evening. Your Granny won't say no. Oh, dear! I've no more change. Phone me when you know about next weekend. I'm glad you're back, and without an American accent."

"Granny says I've caught a lot of words –" But the line had gone dead.

Ten minutes later Rose Conway, another of Drina's great friends, was on the line from Chalk Green, the Dominick Residential School in the Chilterns.

"Oh, Drina! So you *are* back? How lovely! I've hated to think of you so far away."

"It's nice to be missed," said Drina, and meant it, but she was conscious of a faint feeling of guilt. How little she had missed *them* in New York. Walking down Madison … in the Rockefeller Plaza … looking at the wonderful shops on Fifth Avenue … the Dominick and all her friends had seemed in another and less important world.

"How is Chalk Green?" she asked quickly.

"Oh, it's fine. A thousand times better without Christine. We've been out on Wain Hill this afternoon. It was quite warm sitting on Bledlow Cross; all blue-misty, with the trees a wonderful colour. You should see the spindle and the dogwood and everything. But listen … Have you heard the awful news?"

"No. What?" Drina's voice was sharp.

"Well, *you* mentioned it first in a letter, but you didn't believe it. You said it was a silly rumour. But Catherine Colby *is* retiring."

"She *can't* be!" Drina's hand tensed on the receiver. Catherine Colby was the prima ballerina of the Dominick Company and she had been travelling to the States for a holiday on the *Queen of the Atlantic*.

"Yes, it's been in all the papers. Yesterday, I think it was. She's ill. Acute anaemia, the papers said, and she's been having some trouble with her back as well."

"But the Dominick wouldn't be the Dominick without her!"

"No, of course not. But it's true. She's flying back from America next week and will make a few more appearances and then – everyone here feels terrible about it."

Drina felt terrible, too. It was shattering news. Catherine Colby was a very great dancer, and with her husband, Peter Bernoise, had helped to make the Dominick what it was. After Elizabeth Ivory's death the Company had not been so good for some years, until Catherine Colby had brought her wonderful talent and lively personality to grace the Dominick stage.

Drina wandered into the living-room looking so pale and wretched that Mrs Chester was startled.

"What on earth is the matter? Are you tired? You'd better go to bed soon."

"It's not that, Granny. But Catherine Colby *is* retiring. Oh, isn't it a tragedy? I should think it will kill her. It would me!"

Mrs Chester said rather sharply:

"I've told you before that people don't die so easily. It *is* a very great pity, but Catherine Colby has a husband and a beautiful little daughter. The world won't end for her because she has to give up dancing."

Drina didn't argue, but she could not feel that even sweet little Penelope could make up to Catherine Colby for the life of the theatre; for the deep satisfaction of dancing, for the fame and lights and applause. When you had been doing something since you were ten years old and it was taken away from you ... Oh, it was dreadful!

The telephone bell rang again and Mrs Chester said resignedly, "I suppose it's for you. You may as well answer it."

This time it was Ilonka Lorencz, another friend from the Dominick. Ilonka's family were refugees who now kept a restaurant in London, and Ilonka's older sister, Terza, was in the Dominick *corps de ballet*. She had also written a best-selling book, *Diary of a Dancer*, that was soon to be made into a play.

"Oh, Drina! You're back! I'm so very glad!" Ilonka now spoke very fluent English, though with a slight accent.

"Just a very short time ago. I'm dying to hear all the news, but Rose has just told me about Catherine Colby."

"Oh, yes, but it is terrible! Everyone is so upset. Mr Dominick looks years older – yes, really, he looked quite different yesterday."

"But he must have known before that."

"Of course. But yesterday we noticed how he looked. And, Drina, the booking for the new period opened yesterday, so I got seats for her last appearance. I thought that you would wish it."

"Oh, thank you, Ilonka. I suppose I *shall* want to be there," Drina said sadly. "I don't know how we'll bear it, though."

"And you had a wonderful time in New York?"

"Yes, I did. It's the most beautiful place I've ever seen."

"Beautiful?" Ilonka sounded surprised. "You said so in your letter. Mother said she could not imagine it. So noisy and dirty –"

"Oh, it's not! Of course it has slummy parts – all great

cities do – but in every sort of light, always, it was so beautiful –'' And Drina stopped, because it seemed so impossible to make Ilonka see the city she had so recently left. Manhattan fading into the sea on that blue morning …

"I'll tell you when I see you," she said hastily. "I've brought about a hundred postcards with me. Tell me all the other news."

"Oh, well, there is not so much. Your friend Mark has not been very happy. He has found it strange, though I have heard that he is a good dancer. Queenie and Christine – sometimes I could kill Queenie and Christine!"

"So could I," Drina agreed, for she had never got on with Queenie Rothington, and now that Christine Gifford had been transferred from Chalk Green to London the pair were likely to make a formidable combination. "What have they done?"

"They are just themselves. So unpleasant. Saying always such horrid things."

"I can imagine it. What else?"

"Oh, well, people begin to think about the Christmas Show. I do wish that I might have a part.'

"Perhaps you will, Ilonka." But Drina knew that, with so many young dancers to choose from, only a few from each class could hope to dance at the Dominick matinée given yearly by the students.

"Mother would be so pleased. Queenie is sure that this year she will get a good part, because her –''

"Her mother was Beryl Bertram!" Drina chanted with Ilonka, and they both laughed. Queenie never stopped pointing out that her mother had been a dancer, and Drina often wished that she herself had not decided so sternly that she would keep the secret of her own mother's identity to herself. Now Mr Dominick and

Marianne Volonaise knew, and so, of course, did Rose and a grown-up friend, Adele Whiteway, but it was not general knowledge and she did not mean it to become so. But when Queenie got on her high horse it was sometimes remarkably difficult not to shout to all the world that her mother had been one of the greatest of British ballerinas.

Having arranged to see Ilonka the next afternoon, Drina went very slowly to get on with her unpacking. Her head was spinning with the news she had just received and with thoughts of Jenny. Now she seemed well and truly back in her old life, and yet there was so much to remind her of America.

Her new dresses, bought at Saks Fifth Avenue … She hung them up in her cupboard, remembering all the times she had worn them. Then there was the big pile of postcards … booklets about the Rockefeller Centre, the United Nations and other buildings … paperback books …

Even after she was in bed Drina's restless thoughts went round and round. It was so strange not to feel the motion of the ship and hear the creakings and the distant throbbing of the engines. Big Ben sounded unusually loud; normally she scarcely noticed chimes.

Back in London. Back at the Dominick on Monday. Back to hard work and plans for the future.

But she dreamed in a confused way about New York and Grant, hearing his voice so clearly that she awoke in the dark to the harsh knowledge that she might never hear it again in reality.

Life was very odd; very strange. Wonderful things happened … unexpected things … terrible things.

She turned over and concentrated on the wonderful things. It was the only thing to do in the middle of the night.

2
Back to Ballet School

On Monday morning Drina awoke very early and lay thinking, not about the Dominick, but about the recent past. Even though she was home again, even though that very day she would be back at her dancing amongst her friends (and her few enemies), her thoughts still went back to New York. Yolande ... When would Yolande write and tell her how she was getting on, giving her all the news about the dancing school on Madison Avenue, about Madame and the girls? Yolande, who must, at that very moment, be asleep in the little house in MacDougal Alley, near Washington Square, for, of course, it was still night in New York. That was one of the things Drina was constantly doing; asking herself what time it would be the other side of the Atlantic.

And Grant would be asleep in the apartment on Central Park West. If only Grant would write – but of course he never would. He had probably forgotten about her already. She had given him her address, but that had only been because he had said that some day he might come to London again.

Drina forced her thoughts towards the Dominick and told herself that now only work counted. She had missed nearly a whole month of term, it had been a wonderful holiday, and that was the end of it. Or it should have been. But the trouble was that she didn't feel the same person who had gone, almost reluctantly, to America. Falling in love was uncomfortable – and an odd secret to have. Most people didn't even keep it a secret. There was plenty of falling in love at the Dominick among her own contemporaries but it did not seem to Drina as though her own experience had been in the least the same. People like Bella and Meryl and even the superior Queenie giggled and confessed their feelings, which were usually concerned with boys in the upper classes or young male members of the *corps de ballet*.

"Drina, time to get up!" called her grandmother, and Drina sighed and leaped out of bed. It seemed a chilly morning at last, with a hint of rain.

It was strange to be wearing her Dominick uniform again and setting off with her little case, though it would be good to be really at work again. She definitely *would* have to work, because she had probably fallen behind, even though she had attended classes in New York.

Ilonka was standing at the corner of Red Lion Square and greeted her cheerfully.

"Oh, here you are, Drina! I thought that I would wait. Queenie and Christine have just gone on."

"The sweet things!" Drina retorted rather glumly, seeing her two enemies approaching the steps of the Dominick School.

As it happened, Queenie and Christine stopped to talk to Jill and Betty and the four were still standing there as Ilonka and Drina came up.

"Fancy! Here's Drina back," said Christine, with an unfriendly look. "How we have missed her!"

"Nice of you!" Drina said lightly. She was not going to be ruffled by Christine Gifford during the very first moments. "I can't say I missed *you*. I had far too good a time."

"Well, you've missed a month of term," Queenie said nastily. "You'll have a job to catch up, and the Dominick matinée is coming along, too."

"Drina danced in New York," Ilonka said promptly. She was not in the least afraid of Queenie and Christine, unlike Rose, who had hated and feared Christine when she was at Chalk Green. "She went to classes and she also composed a ballet and danced it in a New York theatre."

"Drina's always full of stories," said Queenie.

"But it is true." Ilonka was flushed, and Drina gripped her arm.

"Shut up, Ilonka!" she whispered. "You know what they're like. Let it go."

At that moment Mark Playford came briskly along the pavement. He and Drina had known each other in their Willerbury days and this was his first term at the Dominick.

"Nice to see you back, Drina," Mark said. He looked pale and thinner than she remembered, and it was clear that he was not very happy.

"How are you, Mark?" Drina asked, as they all went into the hall.

"Getting into it now, I think. I hated it at first. The dancing's all right, but – oh I don't know. It's so different from my old Willerbury school. But I've made friends with a boy in my class – Terry Maine."

"Oh, Terry Maine's nice," Drina said, with relief. "I'm sorry it hasn't been so good."

"My fault, I suppose. I couldn't get into the atmosphere and you weren't here to hold my hand."

Drina grinned.

"It wouldn't have helped you much."

She passed her mother's portrait and the ballet shoes in the glass case below it, and at the top of the cloakroom stairs came face to face with Igor Dominick Junior. Igor looked even more handsome and sure of himself than she remembered.

"We-ell, Drina! Back to the fold after your travels? I quite missed you."

"Did you, indeed?" Drina had not yet forgiven Igor for the way he had treated her in Edinburgh, when he had totally ignored her in favour of his French cousin, Marie.

"You don't believe me?"

Drina laughed and was hurrying past him when he put his hand on her arm.

"You've been distinguishing yourself in New York, one hears. Drina turns choreographer!"

"How did you know?" Drina asked, much startled. "It was only a little ballet, anyway."

"Madame Whatever-her-name-is from that Madison Avenue dancing school wrote to Marianne Volonaise and told her all about it. The letter came at the end of last week and Marianne showed it to my father."

"Oh!" said Drina, and went on to the cloakrooms to change into practice clothes. Already, in the midst of her friends, it began to seem as though she had never been away, and yet, alarmingly, she did not feel the same pleasure as usual. The Dominick was the Dominick, of course, and she loved it, but something had happened – she had seen another world.

She threw herself into her dancing and school work and was relieved to find that she had not fallen much behind, but, as the week passed, she was uneasily conscious that things were not quite as they used to be. A dozen times a day she thought of New York, wondering what everyone she had met was doing, asking herself what time it would be there and what the city looked like in the morning … at noon … at dusk. And, curiously enough, everything conspired to keep her mind on New York. Every time she opened a newspaper, it seemed, there was something about it. "How the New Yorkers Live" roared one headline, and she read, with amusement and indignation, an article that attempted to put into a nutshell something that would hardly have gone into a full-length book. How could anyone *say* how several million New Yorkers lived, when some lived in little old houses in Greenwich Village, some in Victorian houses in Brooklyn, like the one where she had gone to tea, and some in sumptuous apartments on the Park, like the Rossiters?

Then, one evening, she had a brief glimpse of the city on television, and on Wednesday morning there was a long letter from Yolande that most vividly brought back Drina's own short, crowded time in America. Yolande was happy with her aunt … she was enjoying her dancing … she liked her new school.

I've missed you a lot, Yolande wrote, towards the end. *I often see things that I know you would like. The weather isn't so hot any more, and the leaves are falling in Washington Square. This morning it was all misty, blue and gold, and I could just dimly see the Empire State Building away up Fifth Avenue. Oh, Drina, you were so good to me. I shall always be grateful. I'll never be afraid to dance in front of an audience again, and it's all through you.*

Do, do try and come back some day.

Love from Yolande

But Drina knew very well that that "some day" might not be until she and Yolande were grown up.

On Thursday Drina went home with Ilonka to tea. In London, too, the weather was colder now and there was a hint of frost in the air. The restaurant called "The Golden Zither" looked prosperous and cheerful and she was very relieved that her friends were now so happy in London. The family's quarters were on the first and second floors and Ilonka led the way up the rather dark stairs. They were met at the top by Ilonka's small black kitten, Binki, and he alone represented Ilonka's happier state. For she had left a much loved cat in Lynzonia and for a long time it seemed that she would never want another pet.

Drina and Ilonka found Mr and Mrs Lorencz and Terza in the living-room, which looked out on a narrow street. They all looked excited and were talking eagerly.

"Has something happened, then?" Ilonka asked, dropping her case and scooping up Binki with one hand.

"Hullo, Drina!" said Terza. "Just at the right moment! Are you going to audition for a part in *Diary of a Dancer*?"

"Why? Is the play going on soon, then? There have been such a lot of delays."

"It's going into rehearsal just as soon as the cast is chosen," said Terza, whose English was now very fluent. "Mr Goldson-Wade was here just now. With luck, he says, the play will open at the Queen Elizabeth Theatre in about a month. Calum Campbell, whom you know, of course, Drina, is to produce, or do you say direct?"

"Direct, I really think," said Drina. "Though I often get muddled. I usually think of him as a producer. Oh,

Terza, that *is* good news! We'll all come to the first night. Though," and she hesitated, "it will be – rather painful in some ways. Especially for you, I should think."

"Oh, now we feel quite removed from the story," said Mrs Lorencz. "And we are very proud of Terza."

When they were seated round the table Terza returned to the subject of her play, the story of which was, of course, the story of the Lorenczs' own escape from Lynzonia.

"Drina, I meant it. I think you should try for a part in the play."

"But, Terza, I can't. I've only just got back to the Dominick, and the play will probably run for years. I've told you before; I'm a dancer and not an actress. Besides, I don't look old enough to take your part. You were sixteen when you came, and I – well, people keep on saying that I look about twelve."

"Yes, you are right, of course. And Mr Goldson-Wade thinks they may have found someone to take the part of – of Terza. How strange it seems! But you could play the part of the younger sister. You are not unlike Ilonka, though your hair is straight and hers is curly."

Drina was silent, conscious of their eyes on her. She had always found their story upsetting, even though it had had a happy ending. The thought of acting it night after night was scarcely bearable.

"Mr Campbell would give you the part without an audition, I think," said Mrs Lorencz.

"No, I'm sorry. I *must* work at my dancing, and the play really might run for years. It's not like being Margaret in *Dear Brutus*, which was only for a fortnight. I really couldn't stand it, anyway. To go through it every night. No, I couldn't."

"If you feel like that, you would be good. But maybe it is asking too much."

Not much more was said, but Drina was left with a faint nagging feeling of guilt. Should she perhaps try for the part? Was it perhaps her duty to show the world what the Lorencz family and others like them had suffered? But she told herself that she had to dance, and Mrs Chester, on hearing what had been suggested, was heartily relieved by her decision.

"No, of course you oughtn't to do it. Besides, the Dominick would probably never agree to a long run. Your dancing comes first and they have the ultimate say in all you do. Think no more about it."

But Drina was still thinking about the play when she sat in the Willerbury train after school on Friday afternoon, turning over the rights and wrongs of her refusal. She felt as though she were shirking something important, and yet common sense told her that she must get on with her training to be a dancer. It was, after all, the career she had chosen, and she was surely entirely justified in pursuing it unswervingly.

The express sped through her beloved Chiltern Hills and then out into the Vale and away towards Warwickshire. Drina, at last pushing thoughts of *Diary of a Dancer* away, sank once more into thoughts of New York and Grant. But even this made her feel guilty, for she had sense enough to know that she could not go on reliving a few happy and crowded weeks.

When she realised that they were due in Willerbury in ten minutes, she started to think about Jenny, wishing that she could feel more pleasure over the visit. Once she had gone back to Willerbury so eagerly, and of course it would be lovely to see Jenny. But it was dreadful to watch the Pilgrims being so brave facing their problems. The worst thing was knowing just how much Jenny hated her new life, with the chance of attending an agricultural college now so much smaller.

Jenny was standing on the platform and Drina's first glance told her that her friend had altered even in the few weeks since their last meeting. Jenny looked taller and thinner and a great deal more than her fifteen and a half years. It was difficult to remember that, not so very long ago, she had been fat and cheerful, taking life with casual happiness.

"Oh, Drina, my duck!" Jenny cried, "I expected you to look so different after being in America, and buying clothes in Fifth Avenue."

"We only bought party dresses," Drina said.

"And no American accent!"

"I don't know," Drina said, rather ruefully. "I often say 'I guess' and 'I don't have', and I've several times been laughed at for saying 'sidewalk' and 'elevator'. It's so easy to catch, and, anyway, I just loved the voices. If you heard Grant's –" She stopped abruptly, but Jenny wasn't listening. She had taken Drina's case and was leading the way to the exit.

"Have you had any tea?"

"Yes, I had some on the train just as soon as it left Paddington. I was so hungry after school."

"Then you can wait till supper? We'll go and talk in my room. Oh, I'm so pleased to see you!"

But on the bus she was very silent, and Drina felt the dreaded shyness creeping over her. Shy with Jenny. It was terrible, unbelievable!

To her relief Mr and Mrs Pilgrim and the four younger boys seemed cheerful enough, but there was no doubt that both Jenny's father and mother looked older and more worried.

Drina told them something about her trip to America, and bits of news about Mark Playford and the Dominick, and then she and Jenny escaped upstairs to Jenny's room.

"I shall be so sorry to give it up," said Jenny, looking sadly round. "But I daren't mention it to Mother. At the new house I'm going to have a tiny little room. You'll have to come and see over it. We're moving a week on Tuesday."

"Oh, Jenny!"

"It's rather a horrible little house," Jenny confessed, staring out of the window. "But we certainly can't afford to keep this one on, so it's no good moaning." She drew up a chair and a stool, and added, "*Now* let's talk. You don't know how I've missed you. I can't say exactly what I'm thinking to anyone else. Only I was afraid you'd be different after travelling so far and meeting so many new people. *Are* you different?"

Drina's eyes fell, but Jenny was reaching for a cushion and didn't notice.

"Yes, I am different, Jenny," Drina wanted to say. "In New York I fell in love and I don't know what to do about it. Sometimes I can't bear the thought that I may never see or hear him again."

But now, in Jenny's presence, she knew that she couldn't say it. Jenny was too busy coping with the very real difficulties of her own life to be told. It was all going to have to remain a secret.

On the whole Drina enjoyed the weekend, though it still hurt her that there was some sort of a barrier between herself and Jenny. On the Saturday morning they did all the shopping and after lunch Jenny took her to the farm just outside Willerbury where she was working each Saturday and Sunday. It was the only thing, she said, that kept her sane during the long, stuffy week at school.

"But couldn't you have worked at your uncle's farm?" Drina asked.

"It's too far away. I should have spent all my time getting there and coming home. Besides," and Jenny's voice grew strained and sad, "they're selling up. I told you they might, and emigrate. Well, they are, and quite soon, too. *Everything's* changing. I don't know how I managed to trust that life would be secure for so long."

"I don't think I ever have. I often expect the worst."

"I suppose it's nice when it doesn't happen! Oh, yes, you've always been different. But I needed a real bang over the head before I realised it wasn't all honey and roses. A born optimist. That was me."

"Things will get better, Jenny. Just *because* you're an optimist and a fighter."

"You don't know how close I've come to feeling beaten," said Jenny grimly, and changed the subject.

It was a beautiful late autumn day and Drina quite enjoyed wandering about collecting eggs and leaning on walls while Jenny, wearing jeans and wellingtons, cleaned out the pigs and, later, the hen-houses.

"What a lady you look!" Jenny mocked. "Shall I ask Mrs Brookes to lend you some old clothes and you can do the ducks for me?"

"No, thank you, Jenny." Drina quite liked farms after her stay at Chalk Green, but cleaning out ducks or anything else held no charms for her.

"Perhaps you're right. It's heavy work. They're mucky things, ducks. But you look as though you're going to dance at any moment. Isn't it strange that we've turned out so different?"

"We were always different, in every way." And they always had been, even when Jenny, to please her mother, had been learning ballet at the old Selswick School.

"And we'll get more so," Jenny stated calmly, as though stating an obvious fact.

"Oh, Jenny, I wish we needn't!"

"No use wishing. It just will be. You're going to be great and famous. You started long ago. I shall never forget how I felt as I watched you as Françoise in *Argument in Paris*. It was even stranger than seeing you dance, sitting there in that West End theatre and knowing that your acting had been reviewed in all the national papers."

"Oh, it wasn't. Only in a few, and not every critic liked me."

"Well, you know what I mean. And since then you've been Margaret in *Dear Brutus*, and Little Clara in *Casse Noisette* at the Edinburgh Festival. And then you've danced in New York."

"It was only a show given by a dancing school."

"It was in a real theatre, though, and you did your own ballet. Oh, yes, we're different. But I hope it won't make any difference to *us*. Do you think we'll still be friends in five years' time?" Jenny leaned on her fork and, though her tone was casual enough, her face was grave.

"Of course we will. We must be. I – I can't imagine life without you somewhere in it."

"OK," said Jenny, picking up her barrow and starting to trundle it away. "I'll hold you to it. *I* sent you to the Selswick School. I always feel I have a little hand in your success. I can't imagine life without you, either."

When she came back she was more light-hearted and started to tell funny stories about the Grossdale.

That evening they went to visit Joy Kelly, whom Drina had known since the days at the Selswick, and they all enjoyed themselves. The next morning Jenny took Drina to see the new house, which was on the other side of Willerbury. It certainly was "rather a horrible little house", as Drina saw with dismay. But

Jenny remarked on its good points: that it was nearer the station and the Grossdale and that the small garden would be easier to keep in order.

After an early lunch she took Drina to the station, on her way to the farm, and they walked up and down the platform in one of the silences that now fell rather too often between them. Finally Jenny said:

"I'll save up and try to come to London after Christmas, but the fare costs such a lot. Write often and tell me all the news. What's the next excitement?"

"I don't really know. The Dominick matinée, perhaps. You can hardly call it an *excitement* going to watch Catherine Colby's last performance."

"No, you'll hate it."

"We all will. The whole school and Company feel terrible about it. Oh, Jenny, here's the train!"

"Give my love to your grandmother and take care."

"*You* take care. Don't work too hard at that awful book-keeping and shorthand."

"I must."

Drina leaned out of the train until Jenny had quite disappeared, and then she sank down in her corner.

"Oh, Jenny!" she thought. "I wish that things needn't have turned out like this for you."

The train gathered speed and rushed through the misty, golden countryside, carrying her back to London and the Dominick and the weeks of work before Christmas.

3

Farewell to a
Ballerina

Catherine Colby returned to the Dominick Company and seats for her last performance were completely sold out. Drina was very grateful to Ilonka for booking for them both so promptly, but whenever she thought of that last performance of all her heart seemed to turn over.

Catherine Colby's lovely lyrical dancing had always been an inspiration to everyone at the Dominick School, and to Drina perhaps more than most. She had, of course, seen many other great ballerinas, but there was something about Colby that had always seemed the very essence of beauty and style.

Drina wondered, as the time drew nearer, how in the world the dancer was finding the courage to face these last few appearances. It must be almost worse than being struck down by some accident or illness before you knew it.

She was wandering across Red Lion Square one morning when she saw a familiar car, and there was Catherine Colby herself, just locking its door and apparently intending to go to the rehearsal room, which was next door to the Dominick School.

Drina stopped abruptly, shy and awkward. They had not met since they had been fellow-passengers on the *Queen of the Atlantic*, and she had been amazed then at the easy friendliness with which the ballerina had treated her. She, unimportant Drina Adams, who was still a junior at the Dominick!

She would almost have been glad if Catherine Colby had not noticed her, but the dancer turned and saw her hesitating there.

"Hullo, Drina! So you're back again? Did you enjoy New York?"

"Oh, yes. It – it was the most wonderful thing that ever happened to me."

"It is a fascinating city, isn't it? And I hear that you did your ballet, *Twentieth Century Serenade*, at the Karne-Lucas Theatre?"

"How – how did you know?"

"Marianne Volonaise told me. She wants to see that ballet one day. It was a very good effort. It deserved a bigger audience than saw it on the ship."

The ballerina and the young dancer looked at each other, and Drina saw that Catherine Colby was very pale (she never wore much make-up off the stage) and certainly didn't look well. Drina thought wildly that perhaps she ought to say something – say that she was sorry about the need to retire. But the words stuck in her throat.

Catherine Colby helped her by saying quite casually: "You'll have heard that I'm retiring?"

"Yes, I – I have heard. I think it's the most terrible thing that's ever happened."

The ballerina actually laughed.

"The world won't come to an end because there's one dancer fewer."

"But you are – *you*. It will be a most dreadful loss to – to the ballet world. Everyone minds very much. I – I mind so much that –"

Catherine Colby put her hand on Drina's arm for a moment.

"Don't take it so much to heart. There are others coming along. Even you."

"*Me*?" Drina's voice was so deeply shocked that Catherine Colby laughed with real amusement.

"Yes, you. You might take my place one day. In how many years? Six or seven? Fifteen, aren't you? You could get quite a long way by the time you are twenty-one."

"But – but I may never even get into the *corps de ballet*!"

"Oh, you'll get into that. Do you still doubt it? I remember the fear I used to feel, in case I wasn't chosen. I know you've a long way to go, but you'll get there. I shall watch your career with the greatest interest."

"Oh, thank you!" It was almost too much, and there were tears in Drina's eyes as Catherine Colby went off towards the rehearsal room.

Drina crossed the road, blinking back the tears, and was aware that students in red and grey were approaching the steps of the Dominick. Amongst them were Queenie and Christine.

"Well, I like your cheek, Drina Adams!" Queenie said. "Fancy going up to Catherine Colby like that – I don't know how you dared. But then you always did think too much of yourself."

"I – I didn't. I just happened to be there and she asked me about New York. She was on the same ship."

"And I suppose you made the most of your opportunities?"

Drina's never-very-deeply buried temper was rising. She stared up into Queenie's face, swinging her case in such a way that Queenie took a step backwards. She had never forgotten the way that Drina had fought her long ago.

"You have a simply wicked tongue, Queenie. Do you ever say anything nice?"

"Not often," said Jan Williams, a boy with whom Drina had always been friendly. "She's the Queen of Cats, as we all know. Take no notice of her, Drina."

"Queenie is just jealous," said Ilonka, who had come up. "Catherine Colby is quite unaware that *she* exists, even if Queenie's mother *was* Beryl Bertram."

"Oh, shut up!" said Queenie rudely. "You're nothing but a refugee."

This time Drina was within an inch of hitting her, but she remembered common sense in time, helped by Jan's restraining hand.

"I hate her!" she muttered, as they walked through the hall. "Horrid, loathsome girl! She gets worse. I think it's having Christine always with her, and Christine is really the nastier of the two.'

"She is jealous," Jan said sensibly. "They both are. I shouldn't let them upset you."

"I do try. But calling Ilonka a refugee –"

"It does not hurt me," Ilonka said calmly. "It's nothing to be ashamed of."

"But it's so mean of her." And Drina was still fuming as she changed into practice clothes and followed the other members of her class up to the studio. Only when her hands touched the familiar *barre*, and the usual exercises began, did she calm down and then she began to feel ashamed that, once more, she had allowed Queenie Rothington to get under her skin.

Catherine Colby's last appearance was to take place on a Saturday evening at the beginning of November, on the day after Drina's fifteenth birthday.

Drina enjoyed her birthday. She was up very early, so that there would be time to open her presents before school. There were plenty of parcels. A pretty scarf from Mrs Pilgrim (fancy her bothering in the midst of so much trouble and hard work!), one of the newest ballet books and a card with a picture of the Royal Ballet dancing *Les Sylphides* from Jenny, talcum powder and soap from Rose of the make and perfume that Drina liked best, a new record case and an expensive record token from her grandfather, and a beautiful pair of fur-lined gloves from her grandmother. There were also piles of cards, including several from Drina's friends at Chalk Green, and a handsome one from Igor Dominick.

Ilonka met her in Kingsway and produced a book token and, wonder of wonders, Marianne Volonaise herself saw Drina in the hall, and said, smiling:

"Many happy returns of the day, Drina."

Drina gaped. *Madam* knowing that it was her birthday!

"Oh, thank you, Miss Volonaise. But how – how did you know?"

"A little bird in the shape of Igor told me. He remembers your birthday because you were so angry when he thought you were only a child, that time in Italy. And as a matter of fact," she lowered her voice, "I think I should have remembered, anyway. Child, I saw you when you were only a day old. Elizabeth Ivory's daughter, remember. I looked at you, so very tiny and dark, and wondered if you would be a dancer, too."

Drina stared up at her wordlessly. It still seemed strange and almost embarrassing that Miss Volonaise now knew she was Ivory's daughter.

"It seems very odd," she got out at last, and Miss Volonaise laughed.

"What? That you were once only a day old? And it occurs to me that *I* called you 'child'. But perhaps you can forgive *me* more readily than Igor!"

"Oh, of course. He's only a boy."

Miss Volonaise laughed again and turned away towards the main staircase.

So somehow the day turned out the happiest one that Drina had spent at school since her return from America. It ended with a birthday tea for herself and Ilonka, and then the two of them were taken to Covent Garden by Mr and Mrs Chester, sitting in splendid seats in the Grand Tier.

"The Opera House tonight and the Dominick Theatre tomorrow," Drina sighed, as they waited for the great red-and-gold curtain to rise on *Sylvia*.

"But tomorrow is not all for pleasure," Ilonka remarked sadly.

Mrs Chester clucked rather indignantly.

"You are a silly pair! I can't imagine why you are going at all, when you know it will only make you miserable."

"But, Granny, we have to be there. We shall never see her dance again."

"Well, you've seen her dance dozens of times, and I know what you are, Drina. It will be an emotional occasion and you'll come back thoroughly upset."

"I can't help it, Granny."

Then the house lights faded and the overture began, and, at the sound of the drums, Drina's whole mind was given over to the coming ballet. Oh, it was wonderful, exciting music! The drums were one of the most thrilling things in the world.

The curtain rose on the scene before the shrine of

Eros and she waited, in an enchanted stillness, for the
entrance of the ballerina. She never cared much for the
dance of the fauns and dryads. It was just a prelude ...
The whole thing was just a prelude until the sound of
the hunting-horns and Sylvia came leaping on to the
stage. *Now*, the horns ... and the drums again. And
Drina had forgotten everything in the world (even
Grant Rossiter, who was generally somewhere in her
thoughts), everything except the ballet before her, with
a dancer who was a good deal greater than Catherine
Colby giving one of her wonderful, unforgettable
performances.

But by the next day her mood had changed and she
found herself depressed and rather dreading the
evening. Perhaps her grandmother was right and it
would have been better to stay away. And yet how *could*
she stay away from the Igor Dominick Theatre that
evening? It was asking too much. If Catherine Colby
had the courage to face the last cheering and the flowers
and the endless curtains, then she, Drina Adams, had
the courage to sit there in the front row of the Circle,
watching it all.

Everyone at the Dominick School had subscribed
towards a huge bouquet. Everyone who could would be
there, but countless fans had been turned away at the
box office. Catherine Colby's early retirement was one
of the saddest and most sought-after occasions of the
ballet world.

It was a Saturday and, as usually happened, Drina
went shopping with her grandmother. In the afternoon
Drina and Ilonka walked right across Hyde Park and
into Kensington Gardens, but it was a faintly
melancholy day, misty and cold, with most of the leaves
already off the trees and the smell of bonfires filling the
air. Not really the kind of day to cheer anyone up.

"How sad autumn is," Drina remarked. "Well, it's early winter now. What a lovely spring and summer it was. It seems so long ago since Italy. It even seems a lifetime since Edinburgh. And I can't believe – oh, Ilonka, only a very few weeks ago I was in New York!"

"You think about it very much," said Ilonka.

"I can't help it. I wonder what it looks like now? I wonder if there are bonfires in Central Park and if the skyscrapers look blue in the mist? Sometimes I wish I *could* forget it. I never knew it was possible to feel so haunted."

"Oh, but I know," said Ilonka, gazing ahead at the rising blue smoke beyond the Round Pond.

"Your old home, you mean?" And Drina's warm heart suddenly went out to her friend. In a couple of short weeks she had learned to love a city, as well as Grant, but Ilonka had lost forever the city where she had been born, and played, and gone to school.

"Yes. Never to go back! It was not happy. I don't want to remember, for now we all like London and everything is well. But often I *do* remember. Often I wish that things might have been different. If Queenie knew what it was like to be a refugee she would not throw – throw the words about so casually."

"I expect she does know, really. It's partly that you don't *look* like a refugee. Terza's made a lot of money, and your father and mother are happy, and –" But Drina painfully remembered her first meeting with the tearful Ilonka in the cloakroom of the Dominick, when it had seemed that Mr Lorencz would never reach the safety of Britain.

"We are so lucky. So many thousands round the world have not been lucky as we are. People in camps ... without any home ... Oh, I can't bear to think! But sometimes I dream of my own city, and then it always seems beautiful, not sad and frightening. Isn't that strange, that I should remember when it was beautiful and forget the – the terror?"

"You make me feel ashamed!"

"But why should you? It is not shameful to think about New York, to love it and want to go back."

"I may never go back. That's really the trouble. If I could have stayed longer ... if I could have got it out of my system more –" For a wild moment Drina thought of telling Ilonka about Grant, but the impulse passed. She said instead, "It's getting late. We'd better nip down the Broad Walk and get a bus near the Albert Hall. We've got to get home, and have tea and change."

They met again at seven o'clock outside the underground station and walked the short distance along the Embankment to the Dominick Theatre. Drina was wearing her emerald green dress, but it did not feel like a festive occasion. She felt rather cold and decidedly apprehensive. The evening had turned clear and the lights across the river sparkled. The Royal Festival Hall ... the lighted buses speeding across Waterloo Bridge ... the cheerful Saturday evening crowds, did nothing to dispel her feeling of melancholy. Now Catherine Colby would be in her dressing-room, and Drina tried to imagine her feelings.

Outside the Dominick Theatre crowds of unlucky people without tickets were hanging about in the hope of getting last-minute returns. Drina and Ilonka pushed their way into the entrance and were greeted by one of the ticket-collectors, who knew them well.

"So you're here, are you? And good seats, too, I see! It's a sad occasion."

"It's awful!" Drina agreed.

"She's a lovely lady. We shall all miss her. Always a friendly word for everyone, no matter how unimportant."

"It sounds almost as if she's dying," said Ilonka, as they climbed the stairs to the Circle.

"In a way she is. After this she'll just be Mrs Peter Bernoise."

"But she'll still be a lovely lady."

"Yes, but it can't ever be the same."

After the rising tiers and great domed roof of the Royal Opera House, the Dominick Theatre seemed small. Every seat was soon taken and people were standing at the back of the Circle. Drina and Ilonka studied their programmes, though they knew already who was dancing the main rôles.

"If it was me," said Drina, "I simply couldn't go through with it. I just shouldn't have the courage. And think what she'll always feel like later when she looks at this programme. 'Catherine Colby as Giselle, Peter Bernoise as Albrecht ...' I wonder how Peter Bernoise feels about it, anyway? After this, he'll be dancing with Renée Randall and –"

"He sometimes has before."

"But not often. He and Colby just *go* together."

Then the house lights faded, the overture began, and the blue curtain presently rose on the familiar set of the two little cottages and the backcloth of hills and a distant castle. There was Hilarion, and Albrecht, disguised as the peasant Loys. Now Albrecht was knocking at Giselle's door. He was hiding and Giselle ...

Then suddenly Giselle was there, young and lovely and eager, appearing as she had done on innumerable other occasions from the cottage door.

But this was the last time.

Drina had seen *Giselle* on a large number of occasions, and the last time had been at the Metropolitan Opera House in New York. Then she had been lost in incredulous enchantment simply to find herself in that famous theatre, though later her thoughts had wandered to Grant; now she could think only of the ballerina on the stage before her.

To Drina there could be nothing worse in the world than never to dance again. She honestly believed that, if she had been given a choice, she would have preferred to die, rather than to live on without ballet. And, watching that beautiful dancing on the well-loved stage, her heart swelled almost unbearably. Who would *think*, seeing Catherine Colby now, that she was ill and perhaps actually suffering?

As the years passed, Drina saw the same ballet danced again and again, in many different theatres and countries, but she never forgot that evening. Every moment, every movement, imprinted on her mind forever.

During the interval she and Ilonka sat almost in silence, and when the curtain rose again on the blue-lit woodland scene, Drina's hands were tightly clasped. But before the end, when Giselle was pleading with the Queen of the Wilis for Albrecht's life, she clutched Ilonka's hand and remained so until the dawn came and Giselle slowly disappeared into her grave.

The blue curtain came swishing down and for a few moments there was absolute silence. And then the cheering began. It ran round and round the theatre in waves of sound, seeming as though it would never end. As the curtain rose and fell over and over again, people leaned over from the gallery and shouted Catherine Colby's name, and Drina was by no means the only one in that deeply moved audience who was in tears. She sat there with the tears pouring down her face, but quite unaware of them, as Peter Bernoise brought his wife forward again and again. And then Colby came

alone, standing before the curtain, and the flowers filled her arms and were heaped in great masses about her feet.

"How can she smile? *How* can she smile?" Drina muttered, convinced that she herself could only have fled from that cheering audience and flung herself in floods of tears in the privacy of a dressing-room. "Oh, Ilonka, I can't bear it! I can't!"

"It is – very moving," said Ilonka, in a wobbly voice.

Even when the curtain seemed as though it were going to stay down, the cheers and clapping and eager calls went on. The house lights were up. Everyone was standing. But no one would go. And in the end Catherine Colby came back. She made a gesture and silence came at once.

"I can only say thank you all very, very much. There isn't anything more to say, except that I shall miss the Dominick and all of you. Goodbye."

Drina stumbled out into the coldness of the open air. The tears were drying on her cheeks and she scarcely knew where she was going. Ilonka had to steer her.

When Drina let herself into the flat, her grandmother met her in the hall.

"Oh, here you are! I was beginning to worry. Good gracious! Your face! I knew you'd be upset, you silly girl! But you'll never listen to me. You're like most young people nowadays. You think you know best."

Drina followed her into the living-room.

"Oh, Granny, I wouldn't really have missed it, though it nearly broke my heart."

"You always exaggerate so."

Drina giggled rather shakily.

"Granny, you'll say that to St Peter at the gates of heaven."

Mrs Chester allowed a reluctant smile.

"How can I help saying it so often, when it's true? And I don't know what would happen if something *really* tragic occurred."

"You always say that, too. But if you'd been there you would have been moved. I'm sure you would. When an audience cheers and cheers ..."

"An audience easily gets hysterical," said Mrs Chester coolly, but she was remembering many nights when an audience had cheered for her daughter, the great dancer, Elizabeth Ivory. "Have a hot drink and go to bed."

Drina obeyed, but it was a long time before she slept.

4

Terza's Play

For some days afterwards Drina was haunted by the memory of that evening, and thoughts of Catherine Colby – now without the dancing that had always been her life – for a short time entirely superseded her memories of New York and the nagging yearning to hear Grant's voice and see his face.

In the middle of the next week she called to see her friend, Adele Whiteway, after school. Miss Whiteway lived in a flat just behind Westminster Abbey, and she had had a considerable hand in advancing Drina's career. Drina had met her first in a bookshop in Victoria Street, and then by accident in a fog, and for some weeks she had practised in the little studio mainly used by Miss Whiteway's niece, Lena, who was also a pupil at the Dominick School.

Adele Whiteway had been a dancer with the Dominick Company in the days when Drina's own mother had been its prima ballerina, but, soon after Elizabeth Ivory's death, she had had an accident which had ended her hopes of finding fame as a dancer. Instead of turning her back on the ballet world, she had carved out another career for herself as a designer and she frequently did the decor and costumes for Dominick ballets.

Drina was, therefore, never surprised to find her friend painting or drawing, and at first she paid little attention to the materials littering the big living-room and to the little model of a stage set on the table in the window. She pushed back her smooth black hair.

"It's seemed ages since I saw you. Except in the distance. I did see you in the stalls last Saturday evening."

"So you were there too?" Adele Whiteway asked, eyeing Drina thoughtfully, and thinking that she looked even paler than usual and somehow subtly different.

"Yes, in the front row of the Circle. Ilonka got the tickets while I was away. I wouldn't *not* have gone, but – but I can't forget it. I thought it was *terrible*. I don't know how she went through with it."

"It's all a very great pity," said Miss Whiteway, "and she has been very brave. It isn't generally known, so don't mention it to anyone else, but there is just the faintest possibility that some day – it may be years – she may dance again. After rest and treatment."

Drina's face showed her sudden relief.

"Oh, I didn't know. Oh, that makes it less bad; just a little. I thought – never to dance again." And then her eyes met Adele's – Adele had had to face just that, with no hope of a future comeback. "Oh, I'm sorry! I – I didn't mean to be so tactless."

"I don't wince every time someone mentions not being able to dance again," said Adele Whiteway lightly. "Once, long ago, perhaps. I can't deny that I did feel as though life was over, and yet I knew all the time, deep down, that it couldn't be. You're afraid it might happen to you, aren't you? But why should it?"

"I don't know. Anything *might* happen."

"You might die tomorrow, or break both your legs, or

any tragic thing. But the chances are that you won't."

"I suppose I'm really afraid of life," Drina confessed. She could usually talk to Adele Whiteway, where she would have been afraid of her grandmother's brisk common sense.

Miss Whiteway was silent for a moment. Then she said, "We all are, I suppose."

Drina stared. She was still young enough to believe that life's problems disappeared with adulthood, or perhaps that grown-up people felt less fear, less hope, less acute pleasure.

"Are *you*?"

"But of course. Sometimes. There's no way out of it. We're all, in our deepest hearts, and sometimes right on the surface, afraid of misfortune, tragedy, even death. But we go on living and mostly enjoy life, and we learn gradually how to take things. If people have a religion, then that helps; if they haven't, then they find a working philosophy. Or they're poor creatures."

Drina frowned. She asked, after a moment, "Do you think that Granny is afraid?"

Miss Whiteway was silent for even longer this time, perhaps mentally reviewing the cool, composed woman who had brought Drina up.

"Undoubtedly, at times. She worries about your grandfather because he isn't always as strong as he might be, and she worries about you. She isn't a selfish person, so most of her fears are connected with those she loves. I've only myself to worry about and only myself to please."

"But you give so much pleasure. With your lovely designs. I think you do please others."

"Yes, but it's a very pleasant, easy way of pleasing. Come and look at this."

Then Drina did cross to the table and stand staring

down at the little model, which showed a backcloth of rather futuristic Christmas trees covered with lights and decorations, and wings adorned with impressionistic holly and mistletoe.

"It's pretty! What is it for? A ballet, I suppose?"

"Not this time. It's for the second act of a children's play. I'm not satisfied yet; I think I'll have another go at those wings. It has a lot of dancing in it, but it's definitely not a ballet. It's to be called *The Land of Christmas*. Mr Dominick is planning the choreography and I'm doing the sets and costumes. See!" She waved several large sheets of drawing-paper under Drina's nose. "That's the backcloth for the first scene of Act One – the children's playroom. I'm stuck on the backcloth for Act One, Scene Two, because I don't want it to look too like the Land of Snow in *Casse Noisette*."

"Oh!" Drina gave the drawings her close attention.

"These are some of the costumes. The author had the idea at first that the play should be vaguely period, but we thought it would be a change to have something absolutely modern. That's the heroine's costume. She's called Jane. That's for Sylvia, the older sister. I've got rather fascinated with it. It's a change from my usual work. Oh, and that's for the holly fairies. I'm having a bit of a job with the Christmas puddings!"

"But – but is it going to be put on for Christmas?"

"They hope so. But there's difficulty in finding a London theatre."

Soon after that Drina said that she must go.

"Granny fusses if I'm too late. She thinks I need a meal after the long afternoon. She never has been keen about the Dominick canteen. She thinks I don't have a nourishing enough lunch."

"How is the Dominick? Wonderful, as usual, I suppose?"

To her immense surprise Drina frowned and, looking down, scraped the carpet with her toe.

"Oh, it's all right."

"Good heavens! I thought you thought it was the next thing to heaven!"

"So I did," said Drina frankly. "Oh, I do still love it, of course, but this term somehow isn't quite right. It's me, I know. I expect it's missing nearly a month. I've never quite got into the swing of things. And then Christine Gifford has come from Chalk Green and she and Queenie make a terrible pair. They're – they're really vicious together, and they don't like me at all. They go out of their way to say horrible things, and we're – I can never quite keep my temper."

"I thought you learned how to cope with people like that long ago?"

"I thought so, too. But together they sometimes really get me down. Ilonka doesn't care, but Rose would if she were here, which she will be after Easter. Her scholarship to Chalk Green finishes then."

"Really, I shan't be surprised if one of those girls gets thrown out one of these days," said Adele Whiteway, who had, in confidence, heard many stories.

"They're careful when anyone in authority is about. Though Christine did get into bad trouble at Chalk Green for the way she was treating Rose in the dormitory. Being so snobbish about her clothes, and laughing at her because her father is a plumber. Things like that."

"Well, they'd better watch. Neither Mr Dominick nor Miss Volonaise like snobbishness or unpleasant behaviour. A little jealousy is inevitable, but not pleasant for all that. Well, goodbye – come again soon."

Drina found that she felt a good deal better about Catherine Colby after the news she had been given, and conversations with Miss Whiteway always made her feel more balanced and in control of her world. But she soon forgot about the plans for *The Land of Christmas* in the much greater interest of Terza's play, *Diary of a Dancer*, which was now cast and in rehearsal.

A young actress of eighteen, Carlotta Wertz, was to play the rôle of Terza. Carlotta herself had been a refugee when she was eleven, escaping from the Eastern Zone of Germany to the Western Zone and then to Britain. Since then she had attended a Stage School and had acted in two long-running plays in the West End. The rôle of the younger sister was to be played by another girl with foreign blood, Giovanna Renti. Giovanna was sixteen, but looked much younger, and, on the stage, would certainly pass for twelve or thirteen.

"But it ought to be *you*, Drina," Ilonka said, when telling Terza's views on the rehearsals. "Terza thinks so, too. Giovanna's good, but it was your part."

"Truly I didn't want to do it, and I don't think they'd have let me, since everyone seems to think that it will run for a long time. Not that anyone can ever really tell, of course, what will be a success." But Drina still had that faint feeling of guilt, as though she had dodged something that she ought to have done.

The feeling added to her slight sense of unrest, but outwardly things went on much as usual, with ballet classes, school lessons, and weekend outings with Ilonka. Often on Sunday afternoons, as the days grew colder, they would turn off the chilly Embankment to look at their favourite paintings in the Tate Gallery. Drina loved the French Impressionists and had a large collection of postcard reproductions. She loved Utrillo particularly and often pored over her many postcards of Montmartre scenes, enjoying the little squares, the narrow back streets, with just a touch of blue here and there, and, so often, a starkly white glimpse of the Sacré-Coeur.

"I love his grey-white walls best of all," she said one day. "He's made Montmartre so real to me. I wish I could go there."

"But you are sure to go," said Ilonka. "Why not? You have seen Milan and Genoa and now New York. Paris is so near."

"It may be near, but I don't know when I shall go, all the same," said Drina, with a faint sigh. "Granny doesn't really like travelling very much."

"You are fifteen. In a year or so, perhaps, you could go alone. Or I with you."

"Do you know, I never thought of that," said Drina, for, though she had gone to Italy without her grandparents, she had travelled each way in the care of an adult. "Of course we *are* growing up."

"Don't you want to grow up, then?"

"I don't really know. When you talk about going to Paris alone it sounds fun, and far better than being dependent on grown-ups. And – and there are other reasons."

For, grown up, she might return to America. But Grant was, after all, about four years older, and by then he would probably have found another girl. The thought was so sharply painful that Drina winced.

"You have a pain?"

"No. No, Ilonka. I was just thinking."

And the continued thinking led her to the conclusion that she had already reached many times before. Even if she had been older, even if Grant had been a Londoner and not a New Yorker, it would have made no difference. Marriage – even boyfriends – were not really in her future plans. Work was the first and should be the only thing until she had seen how far she might go in the ballet world.

But even having reached this conclusion she continued to think, in any spare moment, of Grant and she read the American notes in ballet magazines with nostalgic eagerness. It was something to know what was happening in New York. Yolande's letters, of course, also gave some information, and they came regularly as the weeks passed.

On the day before the opening of *Diary of a Dancer* at the Queen Elizabeth Theatre there was again a thin blue air letter from Yolande. After describing how she had skated in the Rockefeller Plaza, and various other excitements, Yolande wrote casually:

I was walking down Fifth Avenue the other day, and who should I see but your Grant Rossiter. Isn't he good-looking? I didn't think he would recognise me, but of course he saw me a few times on the ship, and saw me dance. He stopped me and asked how I was, and then he asked about you. Thought you'd like to know.

Drina read that short paragraph over and over again. She could *see* Grant standing on the sidewalk, his face perhaps not so brown as it had been when she had known him. "Your Grant Rossiter." But Yolande had, surely, no idea of Drina's feelings?

And for the rest of that day she was filled with a great envy of Yolande, just because she lived in the same city as Grant.

"I'm a fool. I know I'm a fool," Drina told herself miserably.

But the next evening brought the opening of the play and it gave her something very different to think about. Terza had got good seats for her parents, Ilonka and Drina. She had offered to get them for Mr and Mrs

Chester, too, but the Chesters had said that they would go later. Neither were particularly anxious to see a play that was likely to be so serious and moving. Mrs Chester was not a very ardent theatre-goer, in any case, and Mr Chester, left to himself, would always have chosen a musical or a light comedy. It was only because of Drina that they had been to so many serious plays during the past few years, and so long as she had a companion they were more than content to stay at home.

"I'm sure it isn't suitable for you," Mrs Chester said, rather grimly, as Drina appeared in her emerald green dress and a warm coat.

"Granny, I might have been *acting* in it!"

"I still wouldn't have thought it suitable. Well, don't come home upset, that's all I ask."

"No, Granny," Drina said meekly, said goodbye and went down in the lift.

Terza herself was sitting in the front of the stalls, but the rest of their seats were in the front row of the Circle, which gave Drina and Ilonka an excellent view of the audience.

"There is Miss Volonaise!" Ilonka cried, with awe. "Oh, *look* at her lovely dress, Drina! And there's Mr Dominick."

"And Igor!" Drina added, leaning over the ledge in front of her. "In evening dress! How grown-up and handsome he looks."

"And," said Ilonka, turning round to stare round the Circle, "several of the Dominick dancers. Why! There is Catherine Colby!"

"Where?" Drina looked round frantically.

"At the other end of this row. With her husband. She's wearing a blue dress."

"She looks very beautiful," said Drina.

"But for the rest it is a typical first-night audience, I feel sure."

"If I were Terza I should die long before the curtain goes up!"

"Terza said she might. She could eat nothing and was shaking. She said that at least she wished that the critics might all die before they had a chance to write about the play."

"Some hope," said Drina and bent again to study her programme.

The curtain rose on the living-room of the Lorenczs' home in Lynzonia and at once Drina sank down into a complete awareness of the people on the big stage. She had known that it would be upsetting to see her friends' story acted before her eyes, but it was even worse than she had thought.

There they all were, the father and mother, two daughters and the little cat, and the neighbour who was trying to arrange their escape to a free country. Ilonka gave a little gasp at the sight of the cat in the arms of the girl who was playing her own part. The real cat might be alive still, never understanding, as Ilonka had once said, why its mistress had had to go away. A nervous little cat, Ilonka had said, and a much loved one.

The plans were made. The two parties were to leave separately, Terza and her mother, and Ilonka and her father. And at the end of the act came the dreadful parting, but borne bravely because of the hopes for the future.

Terza and her mother left, and the little ballet-dancer sister stood at the window, then slowly and sadly began to dance. But dancing was a thing she could not do again until they were all safe. She took up the cat and rested her face on its smooth fur.

"Oh, Mitzi, I shall never see you again! Oh Mitzi, I

wish I could talk cat language so that you would understand.''

A few moments later the curtain came down and there was complete silence before the applause. Even that sophisticated first-night audience seemed to have been deeply moved and it was a few minutes before the usual bustling of opening chocolate boxes and pushing towards the bar began.

All the Lorenczs were very silent and Drina sat staring unseeingly down into the stalls. Giovanna was very good. She doubted greatly if she herself would have been as good, and yet the nagging thought was ever present. Should I have done it?

The second act was in two scenes; the first at the frontier and the second in Vienna, and the younger sister did not appear. The opening scene of the third act was an audition at the Dominick School (carefully vetted and arranged by Mr Dominick and Miss Volonaise themselves), and the last in Terza's dressing-room before a performance, the first time she was to appear in the *corps de ballet*.

Her mother had gone to meet the little sister at the airport, and suddenly they were in the dressing-room, too. Some of the story was told and all believed that the father would never reach safety. But soon after Terza had left to go on stage a telegram arrived. Mr Lorencz was safe. And, to the faint, distant music of *Le Lac des Cygnes*, the little sister began to dance, this time happily. It was clearly a dance of hope and thankfulness.

The curtain came down and rose again to show the entire cast. But Drina scarcely saw the faces before her. Her eyes were full of tears. It might not be a great play, perhaps, but it was thought-provoking. Terrible, in places, as in that scene of the frontier, and in the last scene when the little sister believed that her father was dead.

She blinked away the tears in time to see Terza moving to go on stage in answer to shouts of "Author!" and with her was the famous playwright who had dramatised her book. Terza looked very pale and very young indeed in her plain white dress, with just a sparkling blue necklace.

"Well, she didn't die!" Ilonka said shakily. "And I suppose that the critics haven't, either."

"Oh, Ilonka, they'll like it. They must! It's so important that they like it."

"*You* know what critics are," said Ilonka, blowing her nose as surreptitiously as possible.

On the way out reporters and photographers stepped forward to speak to the Lorencz family.

"Just a moment! A photograph, please. All of you. Yes, the younger sister in front."

"What were your reactions to the play?" asked one young man, notebook in hand. "It must have been a sad evening, in many ways. Did you feel that the play was true to what really happened?"

Drina stood to one side, sorry that her friends had to face the publicity. But Mr Lorencz was speaking with dignity and the young man's pen was flying over the page.

"Inevitable, I suppose," said Mrs Lorencz, as they escaped at last. "Come on, Drina. We'll take you home by taxi first. Terza won't get away. There's some kind of a party and they'll wait for the early papers. But we – we shall go home."

It was a cold, black night and the streets were shining with rain. They were all very silent as the taxi sped down the Strand and along Whitehall towards Westminster. Drina was tired and shaken, and so, almost certainly, were the others.

She said shyly, as she prepared to dash across the wet pavement:

"I'm glad I was there. I do *hope* the critics like it. Tell Terza – tell her that I almost wish I'd done it. But Giovanna is better."

Drina found that her grandfather had gone to bed and her grandmother was waiting in her dressing-gown, with hot milk and buttered biscuits.

"How did it go? Oh, tears again, I see. What a girl you are!"

Drina gulped the milk.

"Oh, Granny, I really couldn't help it. I'd have had to be a stone statue not to feel moved by it, especially knowing them and everything. Of course it does have a happy ending, and in the actual diary it didn't, because Mr Lorencz didn't really arrive in England for months. Not till I was back from Italy, remember? You will go, won't you?"

"Maybe. If it runs."

"I think it will. There was – there was a sort of atmosphere. You know – as though *everyone* was spellbound. And Carlotta is lovely. It was one of the best performances I've ever seen, as though she was acting with her whole heart."

Mrs Chester grunted. She looked tired and old.

"Get to bed quickly, Drina, and try not to make a noise. Your grandfather seems to be starting some of his chest trouble."

"Oh, dear! I am sorry!" Drina was immediately back to reality.

"Probably nothing much to worry about, but I *do* worry. Now hurry, or you'll never get up in the morning."

5

"The Land of Christmas"

The play *was* kindly reviewed by the critics and all seats were soon booked up for several weeks to come. Drina was glad, for it would mean a good deal of money for Terza, and in any case, it would have been awful to feel the story rejected by the public.

A British film company was interested in the film rights, and for a few days Terza was one of the most photographed girls in London. Ilonka, too, came in for her share of fame and one photographer even penetrated into the Dominick School and asked permission to take a picture of her at the *barre*.

Ilonka was flustered, but Terza took her second taste of fame with calm common sense.

"I am glad. Yes, very glad indeed. It's lovely to make money, and lovely that people understand. But really I'm a hard-working dancer. And next week I appear in my first solo rôle."

"Oh, Terza, what is it?" Drina was having tea with the Lorencz family.

"Prayer in *Coppélia*. I am also soon to dance one of the Blue Skaters in *Les Patineurs*."

"Oh, Terza, some day you may take Catherine Colby's place."

Terza gave a cynical little smile.

"I doubt it. I'm average, that's all. I shall never be a great dancer."

"Then you'll write lots of other books."

"I shall marry and have several children."

"But you can do that as well."

"Drina doesn't think much of marriage," said Mrs Lorencz and everyone laughed. Drina laughed, too, but coloured most unusually.

"Dancing does come first for me, that's all I know."

"You think so now. Wait until you meet someone who helps you to change your mind."

Drina wanted to say, "But I know now. I can see what it might be like. I saw it on the *Queen of the Atlantic*, when I felt so strange and restless; all sorts of feelings I'd never known before." But she remained silent, because no grown-up would believe that a fifteen-year-old could really understand.

The next morning there was a letter from Jenny.

Dear Drina,

How are you? You aren't writing as much as usual, but I suppose you're deep in work, and the first night of Terza's play must have been quite something. We read about it, of course, and saw Terza interviewed on television.

I spent last weekend at my uncle's farm. Probably the last time I shall ever stay there, as they have sold it and are moving out soon. On Saturday evening we all went over to the next farm, Hogdens'. Do you remember how we met that red-haired young man when you had a puncture? Robert Hogden, the farmer's grandson, who is living with them now.

Well, you know I didn't like him at the time, but this time he didn't seem so bad. We went round the farm and had quite a talk and he didn't treat me as though I were just a kid. How I envy him because he's working on the farm all the time!

School is much as usual. The girls can talk about nothing but boyfriends, and new lipsticks and different hairstyles, and pop stars, and the boys are nearly all spotty and stupid. But Timothy is still nice. I went to see a climbing film with him the other evening.

By the way, the Hogdens invited me to visit them any time I like. I didn't see Robert's girlfriend. Perhaps he hasn't got her now, because she wasn't mentioned.

Do write soon and tell me all the news. London feels as far away as Africa. How I loathe shorthand, and bookkeeping is the end!

Love,
Jenny

Drina was still thinking about Jenny when she reached the Dominick School and she was startled out of her somewhat gloomy thoughts by a message brought to the cloakroom by a very junior girl.

"Please, Drina, Madam wants to see you in her office."

Drina, just dressed in practice clothes, finished tying her ballet shoes and looked up, startled.

"Me?"

"Going to give you a dressing-down!" said Christine nastily.

"More likely going to butter her up," added Queenie. "Drina's Miss Volonaise's favourite. We all know that."

Drina ignored them and ran hastily to the cloakroom stairs, up the next flight and along the corridor. In answer to her knock Miss Volonaise herself opened the door.

"Oh, come in, dear. I want to speak to you about your ballet, *Twentieth Century Serenade*."

Slightly breathless from her rush, Drina merely stared at her. Miss Volonaise went on:

"It sounds most interesting. I heard about it from Madame in New York and also from Catherine Colby. I want you to teach it to Ilonka and then give me a special performance. I gather that it is for two girls, and not an ordinary *pas de deux*?"

"That was because I did it for Yolande and me on the ship," Drina explained quickly.

"Well, you and Ilonka may miss your ballet class this morning and I'll send you a pianist along to the little Blue Studio. Perhaps you could work again for half an hour after school and again in the morning? It needn't be perfect. I'd just like some idea of it. We wondered if it might do for the matinée."

"Oh, Miss Volonaise! But it's such a *little* ballet!"

"I gather it went down well on the ship and in New York. Besides, I shall be interested to see your first attempt at choreography." She studied Drina carefully. "You look very pale. Are you all right?"

"Oh, yes, thank you, Miss Volonaise."

"Well, you always are rather pale, except when you get sunburnt. I must warn you that you and Ilonka may not be able to dance *Twentieth Century Serenade* yourselves at the matinée."

Drina's heart sank, but she took what she assumed to be a blow bravely.

"I – I quite understand. You'd want it to be two of the Seniors."

"No, that isn't it at all. I think you may be otherwise occupied. But more of that later. Run and find Ilonka, will you? The Blue Studio. You won't be disturbed."

Drina rushed off – receiving a reprimand in the corridor for her dangerous haste – and hauled Ilonka out of one of the big studios, where she was warming up at the *barre*.

"Come on! I want you. We're let off our class today."

Ilonka followed her without question and Drina led the way to the Blue Studio, which was not in the main building, but across the bare space somewhat optimistically called "the garden" at the back. On the way she explained.

"We're to show it to Miss Volonaise, but she says she has other plans and we may not be able to dance it ourselves at the Dominick matinée. I thought at first it was a gentle reminder that we aren't important enough, but she said it wasn't that. So it looks as though we're going to be in another ballet."

"Oh, Drina, if only we might be chosen! Of course it doesn't matter so much to you. The matinée isn't important to you, when you've danced at real performances."

"I don't know about that," Drina said rather grimly. "Anyway, I feel pretty odd at the thought of my ballet being danced at the Dominick matinée."

She was demonstrating to Ilonka when the pianist arrived with the *Twentieth Century Serenade* music, and at first Drina felt awkward and self-conscious. But Ilonka was a good dancer and very quick to grasp a point and before the hour was over they had run through the whole ballet and it was even beginning to take shape.

"What did I tell you?" said Queenie, who had somehow got wind of what was happening. "Favouritism! None of the rest of us can miss a class."

"None of the rest of you have made a ballet," Ilonka retorted.

Several of the others stared.

"Do you mean that ballet Drina did in America?"

"Yes, and naturally Miss Volonaise wants to see it.

Drina isn't Miss Volonaise's favourite. It is just that she is clever."

"You think yourself someone these days, just because your sister wrote a play about you," said Christine.

But Queenie had seen the play and had been surprised to find herself very moved. She said with unusual asperity:

"Oh, shut up, Chris! Ilonka can't help being in a play. And one of these days *I* shall make a ballet."

Christine shrugged and turned away, muttering some unpleasantness directed at Drina and Ilonka. The rest of the day passed much as usual. That afternoon after school Drina and Ilonka worked again at the ballet, and by the next morning when they had spent a further hour on it Drina said that she supposed it would do, if Miss Volonaise only wanted an idea of it.

She had scarcely spoken when the door opened and Miss Volonaise walked in.

"You haven't had very long, I know, but may I see it now? What did you wear, by the way?"

"Very loose, soft dresses, Madam," Drina explained.

"Yes, I see. Well, practice clothes will have to do now. May we have the music again, please?" she said to the pianist, and Drina and Ilonka, flushed and rather anxious, took their places. It was a terrible ordeal to dance alone in front of Miss Volonaise, and one, of course, that happened to few girls of their age.

It was worse for Ilonka, in one way, as she had not had Drina's experience, but Drina was suddenly painfully conscious of the imperfections of her little ballet.

She spoke a few words of explanation and then the music began. Miss Volonaise watched intently, leaning against the piano, with her coat draped over her shoulders in the way that she often wore it. At the end she nodded thoughtfully.

"Yes, I see. A very creditable attempt. It has meaning and charm and some very good choreography. I think it will do splendidly. We'll put it on the programme and I do congratulate you, Drina."

Drina, flushed and with untidy hair, said shyly:

"Oh, thank you, Madam!"

"We'll wait a few days. Mr Dominick and I may have something important to say to both of you. If you can't do it yourselves, Drina will have to teach it to two of the other girls. But we'll see."

Drina and Ilonka, puzzled and excited, walked back to their English class wondering what the future was likely to hold. It was all rather mysterious.

In a very few days' time they knew. Mr Dominick appeared one morning at a special assembly of the middle school and explained about *The Land of Christmas*, and how it was to be put on over Christmas in the northern cathedral city of Francaster, at the Royal Crown Theatre.

"We weren't able to get a London theatre for it," he said. "But Francaster has always been a very theatre-conscious place, and we feel that it may be a very good thing to try the play out there this Christmas. It will open a day or two before Christmas Eve and will run for a couple of weeks into the New Year. It is a play with plenty of dancing in it, and some singing. Some of the dancers will be children from a local ballet school, but we plan to take the principals from here."

An excited buzz started, but he held up his hand.

"The play is about two children who go to the Land of Christmas. The leading parts are Charles, the boy, who has the idea that Christmas all the year round would be a wonderful thing, and his little sister, Jane. There is an older sister, Sylvia, who also has a good part, and an older brother, William. The parts of the father and mother will be played by quite well-known actors and actresses, and the same goes for the parts of Father Christmas and of the Midnight Witch.

"We plan to hold an audition tomorrow afternoon, so anyone whose parents would be willing for them to go to Francaster may attend. We shall want a Chrismas Tree Fairy, the Fairy of the Forest – she is the Midnight Witch's attendant – and leaders for the Plum Pudding Fairies and Elves, the Holly Fairies, the Mistletoe Fairies, and so on. But don't come if you can't sing. I hear from the singing mistress that we have some quite good voices in this part of the school, so I have hopes. Any questions?"

There was silence at first and then Queenie put up her hand.

"Yes?"

"Please, Sir, you didn't mention auditioning for the main parts of Charles and Jane and Sylvia and William."

Mr Dominick smiled.

"No. We have more or less made up our minds whom we'd like for those parts, but later we'll audition for understudies. They will have to come from the other dancers taken to Francaster. Is that all? We'll put up the time of the audition on the noticeboard. It will be over in the rehearsal room, no doubt. Thank you." And he walked rapidly away, an awe-inspiring figure to most of them.

Queenie said crossly when he had disappeared:

"*Some* lucky people are going to get those leading parts! Dear little Drina, I bet, for one!"

Drina's heart leaped guiltily. Perhaps that was what Miss Volonaise had meant. But she didn't even know if she wanted to go to Francaster with *The Land of Christmas*. A children's play sounded – well, childish, after turning down the chance of being in *Diary of a Dancer*.

She was not left long in doubt. She was called to Miss Volonaise's office before break, and found Mr Dominick there as well.

"Drina, we want you to take the part of Jane. Miss Whiteway has told us that you know about the play already, and she herself thinks you would be ideal."

"But – but I'm not a singer."

"Well, we hear that you have a very pleasant, tuneful voice. And Jane has the most dancing." Mr Dominick looked shrewdly at Drina's downbent face. "We thought you'd be very pleased. Don't you want to go to Francaster? It would be an interesting experience for you and you would be well-billed. You're quite well-known now after those West End appearances and dancing at the Edinburgh Festival."

Drina hesitated. She felt that she must tell the truth.

"I still feel guilty about *Diary of a Dancer*. Terza wanted me to have the part of Ilonka. I – I keep on thinking that I should have done it."

"We heard about that. You were wise to turn it down. It would have interrupted your dancing for too long. But this will be mainly in the Christmas holidays, apart from a few rehearsals here in London."

"But – this sounds awful cheek – but a *children's* play!"

Both the great ones laughed and Drina flushed, but stood her ground.

"I – I'd really sooner do something *serious*."

"But it's a very charming play, with really tuneful music. You'll like it and we feel sure it will catch on and perhaps be done in London next year. We want you, Drina, if your grandparents will agree. There's another thing which may perhaps appeal to you."

Drina looked enquiring and he went on:

"The Royal Crown Theatre in Francaster is a very beautiful little theatre, and in the past it has put on some wonderful plays. There is a chance that this may be the last show ever to go on there. The lease is up soon and, though everyone in Francaster is fighting hard to save it, it does look as though the theatre may have to go to make way for offices."

"Oh! I always hate to hear of a theatre closing! It – it always seems terribly sad."

"Well, why not go and help in the fight? There *is* just a chance," he said, knowing full well that Drina could not resist the suggestion. A theatre in danger was likely to appeal to what he knew was her romantic nature.

"I will, then, Mr Dominick. And thank you *very* much. I didn't mean to be ungrateful. There's just – one other thing."

"What is that?"

Drina was now very flushed and rather unhappy.

"You haven't chosen me because – because of my mother?"

"We have not. Put that idea out of your head for all time. We want you because you're the best person for the part."

"Then it's all right." And Drina escaped with very hot cheeks.

Half an hour later she learned that Jan Williams was to be Charles, a boy from the class above had got the part of William, and Queenie Rothington was to be Sylvia.

Queenie, who twenty minutes before had been furious to hear that Drina was Jane, was almost completely mollified.

"Of course I have a really strong voice and I look too old to play a child like Jane. Miss Volonaise said that no one else would be right as Sylvia. She *begged* me to take it."

Most people were somewhat unwilling to imagine Miss Volonaise "begging" anyone, but Drina remembered charitably that Mr Dominick had been very persuasive to *her*. She was glad that Queenie was now in such a good temper, but heartily dismayed to realise that they would have to work closely together.

Mrs Chester, on hearing the news about a Christmas in Francaster, was dismayed and rather cross.

"Oh, I suppose you'll have to go, since it all seems to be settled. But I wonder when we shall have any peace?"

"I'm fifteen now, Granny. I don't need someone with me all the time. And the others will be staying in digs, I suppose. I can go with them."

"In theatrical digs over Christmas! I'm sure you'd hate that, and in a strange town, too. Not that Francaster isn't a charming city. I visited it once when Betsy was in the Dominick *corps de ballet*. They danced at the Royal Crown. No, we'll all stay at the big hotel there over Christmas. Afterwards perhaps you can join the others. Your grandfather won't be able to be away very long and I hate him being here alone."

"Oh, *thank* you, Granny!'

Ilonka was rather cast down until the results of the audition were known and then she found herself with the part of the Christmas Tree Fairy.

"Oh, Drina, isn't it wonderful? I shall be a real professional. I shall have to have a licence. And we'll be together."

Others who were going to be in the play were Betty and Jill, Bella and a few of the boys, and Christine Gifford was the Fairy of the Forest. Drina was really dismayed by this news and found herself looking forward to Christmas with little pleasure. Christine *and* Queenie in Francaster! It was too much!

6

A Theatre in Danger

December was a very busy month for everyone at the Dominick. With so many of the good dancers from the middle school going to Francaster there was more opportunity for others to have parts in the Dominick matinée and excitement ran high.

There were, of course, all the usual school activities as well, not to mention end-of-term examinations coming along.

The weather turned very cold and sleety and a good many students were ill, but were back as soon as possible. No one wanted to miss a single minute of the remaining weeks of term.

Drina did not get a cold, and would have been utterly dismayed if she had had to stay away from school, but during the first week or two of the month she was not very happy. She hated the cold, dark days and early dusks and thought often of the delights of summer, and at first she was very unenthusiastic about *The Land of Christmas*.

She had seen *Diary of a Dancer* twice more by that time and was more than ever sorry that she had not tried to be in the play. But she had to admit to herself that it really looked as though it would run for a long time, and though the part of the younger sister was not a large one, it would undoubtedly have tied her more than would have been approved by those in authority.

It was Miss Whiteway who first played her some of the music from *The Land of Christmas* and certainly it was catchy and tuneful. Drina soon found herself singing the songs about the flat, and Mrs Chester grew rather tired of so much repetition. But, even so, it was quite a time before Drina felt in any way caught up in the play.

The early rehearsals were held in a rather sketchy fashion, but, as the month passed, a theatre was found where there could be a short morning rehearsal every day. At the first rehearsal the Dominick dancers met the principals. They all liked the well-known character actress, Yvette Farthingdale, who was to play the Midnight Witch, and also the two who were to take the parts of the father and mother.

Then suddenly, as the play started to be pieced together, Drina began to get an inkling of its atmosphere and to look forward to the rehearsals and the coming run with more pleasure. It was, after all, exceedingly good to be in a theatre again and the director of the play, Matthew Moon, was a man of great character and used to handling young people. Drina liked him and found no difficulty with her part, though at first she found singing, as well as acting and dancing, rather strange.

The final rehearsals would have to be held in Francaster, since many of the dancers were from that city. Igor Dominick had already been up North to teach the dances and Mr Moon and the ballet mistress who had been engaged for the show travelled up to Francaster to see how the work was progressing. They came back saying that they were a good bunch of kids and there should be no difficulties.

Mr Dominick, who had attended many of the rehearsals, got Drina alone one morning.

"Like it better now, do you? Glad you didn't refuse?"

"Oh, yes, Mr Dominick. I can see that it's got something. I shall probably end up by loving it and being very sorry when it's over."

"It ought to go down well," he said. "I'm told that bookings have gone very well already. We'll get you all up there a few days before the opening and it will mean rehearsing most of the time, but you're used to hard work."

Because of Francaster they would miss the last day or two of term, though not the Dominick matinée which was held rather earlier than usual that year.

"We could have been in the matinée as well," Christine said, in her usual disgruntled voice.

"Oh, we couldn't," Jill argued reasonably. "We've had quite enough to do as it is. Thank goodness the exams are over! How I hated that maths paper. They shouldn't expect dancers to have brains as well as bodies."

"You know what importance they attach to *intelligent* dancers," someone said mockingly.

"Then it's too bad. I've mucked up that paper and probably several of the others. But I did a simply overpoweringly intelligent essay on the theatre in Shakespeare's time."

"That's what *you* think!"

Rose, to Drina's delight, had a leading part in one of the ballets for the matinée. It seemed a long time since their last meeting. Chalk Green had had no half-term holiday, largely because there had been a 'flu epidemic.

In spite of Ilonka Drina felt curiously lonely these days. The knowledge that she and Jenny seemed to have drifted apart was always somewhere at the back of her mind, and she was shocked to find that she was almost relieved that they would not, after all, be able to meet after Christmas. Jenny! Poor Jenny! Her life had altered so much that it had apparently altered *her*. Jenny had always been Drina's confidante, but now Drina felt that she could no longer tell her her troubles and deepest feelings. They seemed small indeed beside Jenny's own problems.

Ilonka was sweet, but in many ways she was young for her age, in spite of all that she had gone through. Rose was not, and it was the greatest relief and pleasure to meet her for a brief lunch before the matinée and to find her just as usual, only, if anything, prettier. Rose was thinner and a little taller, but her pallor was a healthy one nowadays, her eyes were bright and her brown hair soft and wavy.

Rose had come up in the Chalk Green special bus, but had permission to escape for an hour or two, so long as she was at the Dominick Theatre in plenty of time.

"Oh, Drina, it seems such years! I haven't properly heard about America, and I shall miss you so during the holidays. If only they'd given us Chalk Greeners a chance to go to Francaster!"

"I did ask once and was told that it had been considered too difficult. We've been needed here nearly every day lately for rehearsals. But, oh, Rose, I do wish that you were coming, too!"

"You'll have Ilonka and all the others."

Drina frowned.

"Queenie and Christine, don't forget. You wouldn't have liked that, especially being in digs with them. And, do you know, Christine's my understudy."

"Really? She'll push you under a bus."

"I shouldn't be at all surprised. She really hates me. More than Queenie does. But at least I think I'll be back well before you return to Chalk Green. The play finishes on January 14th and you don't go back until about the 20th, do you?"

"The 21st. But I *shall* miss you. Home does seem so small and cramped, though I try so hard not to let Mum know." Rose lived in a small house at Earls Court with several brothers and sisters, and there was no doubt that it was a squash. After the beauty and space at Chalk Green Manor it was no surprise that she felt the change, however glad she was to see her family again.

"At Easter you'll be home for good."

"I know. I shall miss Chalk Green. But in some ways it will be really great to get back to the Dominick and to have London to play with."

"It's getting late. We'll have to dash! Oh, Rose. I'm beginning to feel nervous."

"Because of your ballet? But it's sure to be all right. I'm dying to see it. Who's doing it?"

"Meryl and Lorna. Miss Volonaise seems pleased, but I'm still scared."

However, Drina enjoyed the matinée and her ballet was quite a success. It was a peculiar feeling to sit up in the Circle and watch her own choreography.

Then came the business of packing to go to Francaster. Mrs Chester and Drina were travelling together, to stay at the Royal Hotel, but Mr Chester was unable to join them until the day of the first performance. Queenie's parents were going, too, and they would be staying at the same hotel. Neither Queenie nor Drina, naturally, was pleased about this.

Through all the bustle Drina still found herself thinking about New York. Yolande's latest letter spoke of biting cold and a promise of snow, and then Drina saw in a newspaper that New York had had its heaviest snowfall for years. Traffic in the city was almost at a standstill, there were great drifts in Central Park, and motorists were stranded everywhere in the surrounding country. She found that she could see it almost as clearly as though she had been there in such weather. She could stand, in imagination, at the window of the Rossiters' apartment on Central Park West, seeing the snow-covered park, the heavy trees and the great dark frieze of midtown skyscrapers against the lowering sky.

On the evening before they left for Francaster she actually saw New York briefly on television and the sight of the people battling through the snow gave her a very strange feeling. How odd if, in spite of all the millions of people in New York, she were to see Grant! But of course she didn't and the scenes were gone in a flash.

A number of Christmas cards and presents had arrived already, but there were plenty more to come. Mr Chester promised to send on everything that came soon and to bring the rest with him.

"But some things may actually come after you've left!" Drina groaned.

"Then we'll ask the hall porter to re-address all but the largest parcels. Don't worry," said her grandfather.

Not to anyone could Drina confide her hope that Grant might at least send a card. Even a single word from him, a single gesture, would be worth all the other cards and presents. Her longing to see and hear him had not passed, as she had sometimes assured herself that it would.

The morning that they left for Francaster was bright and sunny, though very cold, and icy winds whistled along Platform 14 at Euston Station. A good many parents were there to wave off their dancing sons and daughters, and Queenie was there with her parents. Her father was a plump, undistinguished little man and her mother, the once fairly well-known dancer, Beryl Bertram, was a faded, slightly depressed-looking woman. Looking at her own smart grandmother, Drina was, for the first time, a little sorry for Queenie. It must be awful to have such dull-looking parents! In a way it was pathetic, too, for Queenie was so proud that her mother had been a dancer.

Christine joined the Rothingtons and Drina heard a few words that made her realise for the first time that Christine was spending Christmas with them at the hotel. Drina wished passionately that she had begged to have Ilonka to stay with *her*, but at least they could spend a good deal of time together.

Drina and her grandmother, the Rothingtons and Christine were travelling first class, but the rest of the Dominick crowd, in charge of an elderly woman called Miss Barlow, were travelling second. Drina had protested fiercely about her grandmother's choice, but Mrs Chester, who rather disliked train travel, had been adamant. However, when she was settled with her magazines and newspapers she said to Drina:

"You go along and join the others, if you like. But come back before lunch."

So Drina and Ilonka spent most of the journey talking together and looking out at the wet and wintry Midland fields, gleaming faintly in the December sunlight.

"It's really a first taste of going on tour," said Drina, and felt a sudden twinge of excitement and anticipation. Francaster ... a lovely little theatre that might be doomed ... a new play ... her name well-billed.

"Not for you," said Ilonka. "For you the Royal Hotel."

"Only until after Christmas, and there's no need to rub it in. Granny wouldn't listen, but I'd almost sooner have been with the rest of you all the time. I hate being different."

"You will always be a little different because you are you," remarked Ilonka.

"I don't see why. I'm sure I don't want to be."

Francaster was beautiful. Drina knew that as soon as they drove from the station through the bright, bitterly cold afternoon. It was a little city within sight of the hills of North Wales, built mainly of red sandstone, though there were a number of ancient half-timbered houses. The Romans had had an important camp there and the four main streets were entered by what had once been gates in the thick red sandstone town walls. From the station Drina and her grandparents drove through the East Gate and past the Cross into Westgate Street, where the Royal Hotel was.

Drina's room looked out into the street, already growing shadowy as she began to unpack. With rapidly increasing pleasure, she looked out at the old houses opposite, and at a strange old covered way called a Row. She loved history and old cities, even though she had given her heart to the soaring concrete and glass and steel of New York, and, looking down into Westgate Street, it was not difficult to picture the marauding Welsh storming Francaster.

She longed to go out and explore at once, but her grandmother said it was too cold and too dark and that she must rest before the hard work of the next few days. So it was the next morning before she saw the red sandstone, partly Norman cathedral in Northgate Street and was able to slip into some of the ancient Rows and narrow alleyways.

The first rehearsal had been fixed for eleven o'clock, but Drina was there early. The Royal Crown Theatre, at the top of Northgate Street almost under the city wall, was not difficult to find and *The Land of Christmas* was well-billed already. She stopped to look at the posters, seeing her own name with a sort of wonder. She had not yet grown used to the touches of mild fame that had come her way.

The stage door was down a narrow side street and she entered tentatively, looking into the tiny office. An elderly man, with tufty white hair and nothing like the usual number of teeth, grinned at her.

"Good morning, I'm Drina Adams. May I go in?"

"Yes, do, love. A few of the local children have arrived, but you're the first of the London lot. Mr Dominick was in last night and the director, Mr Moon."

Drina wandered off down the long, dim, dusty passage, sniffing the air as she always did backstage. It was a lovely smell!

The sound of voices led her to the wings, and the group of young people chattering under a working light on the stage stopped talking and looked at her curiously. Drina was not shy and she said cheerfully:

"Hullo! I'm Drina Adams."

"The one who's playing Jane?" There was a faint trace of awe in the girl's voice. She was younger than Drina and she wore tights and a blue jersey.

"Yes."

She talked to them for a few minutes and then wandered away, wanting to see more of the theatre. There would be time to change when the others came. It was still early.

She found the pass door ajar and stepped through into the auditorium. She stood in a side aisle, staring about her, and knew at once that Mr Dominick had spoken no less than the truth. Even in the dim light she could see that the theatre was beautiful. An elegantly shaped little auditorium, decorated in red and gold; a theatre that was alive and used now, but that might so soon, apparently, be cold and dead.

It was a terrible thought and she caught her breath, resolving to find out more about it. How *could* people close theatres, especially beautiful ones? It seemed to her the worst sort of vandalism.

But soon she had little time for thinking. More and more people began to arrive. Mr Dominick was there, Mr Moon, the principals – who were staying at the other big hotel, the White Hart – and the Dominick dancers. Drina joined her friends and they hastily changed into practice clothes in one of the bigger dressing-rooms. Later Drina was to share a small one with Queenie, Christine and Ilonka, an arrangement that pleased none of them.

The rehearsal went on until late afternoon. Most of the cast had brought sandwiches, and hot drinks were carried in from a nearby café. At last the play was really taking shape and all the principals had got the feel of it. The local children, at first awed and rather stiff, gradually relaxed and became part of the whole. It was stimulating and satisfying and Drina was happy to be working hard on a stage again, helping to create something that would have a brief reality.

And so it went on for several days, often until after dusk fell when they all scattered to rest or amuse themselves. Several times Drina went home with the other Dominick dancers, who were living in a street not far from the cathedral, in two big Queen Anne houses that had seen better days but were still comfortable enough. In one of the houses a sitting-room had been set aside for them all, where they could do more or less what they liked, and here, in the evenings, they gossiped and played games.

This seemed to Drina much more fun than being at the Royal Hotel, and she felt guilty about the long hours that her grandmother was spending alone. But Mrs Chester said she was having a good rest and Drina didn't even dare to hint that she was not really grateful for the stay at the hotel. Though it was a big place, she could not really avoid seeing Queenie and Christine and she found their presence vaguely unpleasant and embarrassing. Christine never lost an opportunity to say something nasty, but Queenie was haughty and mainly silent.

"That Gifford girl really is unpleasant," said Mrs Chester one evening. "She has shocking manners, too. I don't wonder that you don't get on with her."

"And Queenie? What do you think of her?" Drina asked curiously.

"Not quite so bad, surely? Christine makes her worse. Mrs Rothington seems rather a poor thing. I had coffee with her the other morning and she talked of nothing but her ailments. I always dislike people who talk about their most intimate symptoms," Mrs Chester said with distaste.

"Can you imagine her being a dancer, Granny?"

"Only because I once saw her dance. Believe it or not, she was once quite good-looking and seemed perfectly healthy."

Drina shivered.

"Could Catherine Colby ever grow like her?"

"I doubt it. She's a woman of spirit and imagination. Beryl Bertram was never a top-ranking dancer, anyway."

Before many days had passed Drina knew all about the situation of the Royal Crown Theatre, or, at any rate, as much as was necessary. The lease was up and the site much sought after for shops and offices in a city where land within the walls was at a premium. There was an eager, enthusiastic pressure group, however, that was fighting hard to save it and Drina offered to help. Already she loved the theatre and could not bear the thought that when the curtain came down for the last time on *The Land of Christmas* it would never, never rise again on any show.

In any spare time that she could snatch from rehearsals in the daytime she gave out handbills begging passersby to do all they could to save the theatre and even insisted on going to a couple of protest meetings. Mrs Chester was dismayed and rather cross.

"I know how you feel, but you've got enough to do without parading about in the cold. It's a pretty little place and was famous in its day, but one can't stand in the way of so-called progress. Look at the St James's Theatre in London. Many famous actors and actresses did everything they could, but down it came and an office block rose in its place."

"I know, Granny. I've heard about that, of course. But perhaps we can stop the Royal Crown going the same way. When the show opens we're going to have a big book in the foyer and everyone will be asked to sign."

"It won't do any good."

"It might. The Arts Council has promised to help. The worst thing is that the theatre hasn't been making much money lately, but if the Council *does* give a grant –"

"You were always a dreamer," said Mrs Chester, "but don't be too sad when it all comes to nothing."

"I shall be sad. I shall feel dreadful. I would over *any* theatre."

"At the rate they've been closing all over the country you ought to spend your days in mourning," said her grandmother, in her sharp, dry way.

But in spite of these comments, and others like them, Drina went on hoping that one theatre, at least, might be saved.

7

Christmas in a Strange City

Francaster began to look very Christmassy, especially as the weather had turned frosty and the sun shone during the short hours of daylight. The shops were colourfully decorated and there were many Christmas trees about the city. There was one outside the cathedral and another inside the building on the west steps, where there was also a Christmas Crib. Drina loved the cathedral and often slipped in for a few minutes before a rehearsal. Before the Reformation it had been a great Abbey and many of the monks' buildings still remained. She loved the quiet arched cloisters, the little garden with the fish-pond, and the soaring Early English chapter-house. But she had not yet had time to explore every corner and promised herself that she would do so when the play opened.

When the play opened! That, of course, was the important thing. She looked forward with some dread and a good deal of excitement to the first night on the Tuesday of Christmas week. Everyone else was excited, too, and some, including Ilonka, were very nervous.

"You needn't be," Drina said to her friend, as they

walked along Northgate Street one afternoon. "You're just right as the Christmas Tree Fairy."

"But it is the first time. You are used to it. Do they have critics here?"

Drina laughed.

"It may be darkest England, but I bet they do. Critics will come from other places, too; I heard Mr Moon saying so. From Liverpool and Manchester and even London."

"That makes it worse, then. I shall be so glad when the first night is over."

The rehearsals with the orchestra went off well and so, on the whole, did the dress rehearsal. Now Drina was really caught up in the magic of the play and was thoroughly enjoying her part. Even Queenie was bearable enough on stage, for she had proved herself quite an able actress and did not carry her dislikes into the actual play. But in the dressing-room she and Christine together were a decided cross to bear.

Mr Chester had sent on a good deal of Christmas post and there were cards on every available surface in Drina's bedroom. There was one from Yolande, who had also sent a wonderful picture of New York and a long letter, but there had been nothing from Grant. Hoping against hope for a word from him, Drina often lectured herself severely.

"Silly girl! He's forgotten you. You know he must have done. But if only he'd sent just a card!"

Three hours before the opening of the play Drina and her grandmother went to the station to meet Mr Chester, and his train was only five minutes late. He appeared smiling and looking quite well, and Drina's heart was filled with affection for him. After all, it was nice to have her own family there for Christmas.

When he entered the hotel lounge before their very

early dinner he tossed a bundle tied with string to Drina.

"More post! What a lot of friends you must have."

Drina opened the bundle with elaborate unconcern, but her heart was hammering. She looked through the cards and letters hastily, but there was no American stamp. Only two Italian ones, and these turned out to be letters and cards from her Cousin Antonia and her Aunt Giulia, who lived in Genoa. Antonia wrote that they had sent Drina's presents separately and Mr Chester confirmed that some large Italian parcels had arrived at the flat.

"There are three," he said. "One is, I think, from your grandmother in Milan. But they were too big to bring, so you'll still have some Christmas excitement when you get home."

Drina was restless and uneasy and could not eat much, and Mrs Chester was, as usual at such times, rather cross with her.

"How can you expect to last through a long evening without some food in your stomach, you silly girl?"

"I'll take some biscuits and chocolate. I'll eat something in the interval if all goes well."

"And if it doesn't you'll starve?"

"I shall probably be sick," Drina said ruefully.

"It's almost sure to go well. The theatre is fully booked and the audience will be in a Christmas mood."

"The critics won't."

"No. I doubt if they know how to be in a Christmas mood," Mrs Chester agreed, suddenly smiling. "Still, starving yourself or being sick won't help. You think the play good, don't you?"

"I think it's lovely. Oh, Granny, you don't know how exciting it is to see something take shape and grow real. All the moves fixed, all the lighting arranged, everything. In some ways it's more exciting than ballet, though I never let myself think that for long. I don't *want* to be an actress. Oh, there really are some great moments. The snowstorm and then the haunted wood, and the moment when Charles and Jane realise that they may have to stay in the Land of Christmas for ever. There's a gorgeous moment when the Midnight Witch is overpowered and the Fairy of the Forest is released from her enchantment. It may be Christine, but she *is* rather good. And then the end of the final scene, when we're all singing by the Christmas tree."

Mr Chester wanted to call a taxi for Drina, who, of course, had to be at the theatre early, but she firmly refused.

"Ilonka's coming for me, and it isn't far. Walking will shake down some of my nerves."

Drina and Ilonka walked briskly past the Cross and up Northgate Street, passing the winking lights on the tree by the Cathedral Gate. In the distance a band was playing "See Amid the Winter Snow" and Drina suddenly remembered other Christmasses and how she had sometimes joined in the carol-singing round the big tree in Trafalgar Square. It was strange to be in another city; oddly dreamlike. And then her thoughts flew, unbidden, to New York, where Yolande might be standing in the Rockefeller Plaza under another tree, with the brilliantly lighted skyscrapers all around and snow underfoot.

"But it's only about half-past one there," she told herself. "Today hasn't really got very far there yet."

"What did you say?" Ilonka asked, looking at her curiously.

"Nothing. Talking to myself. Oh, Ilonka, I do feel odd!"

"I don't see why you should."

"Good gracious! I shall probably have first-night nerves until the end of my life. It isn't really a thing you grow out of."

At the theatre there was a small pile of cards and messages for Drina, including one from Rose and another from Jenny. Jenny's said, "Thinking of you. Good luck." And Drina felt guilty because she had not been thinking of Jenny, and sad, too, because of the gap between them that was nothing to do with distance.

But she soon forgot everything in the special thrill of a theatre come fully alive. Electricians and stage-hands hurried about, there was a good deal of noise and chatter and a tense atmosphere of expectation.

Drina's costume for the play was a red party dress and she had no changes, though the snow fairies brought her a lovely little white cloak to wear on her journey to the Land of Christmas. She was soon dressed and made up and wandered out on stage, where the set for the first act was already in place. Almost the first person she saw was Adele Whiteway.

"Oh, you're here! Wonderful!" Drina cried. "Are you staying over Christmas?"

"Yes, but I couldn't get in at the Royal. That red dress does suit you. I designed it especially for you."

"And the lovely cloak! It's so pretty."

"*You* look pretty green," her friend said, surveying her. "Or would it be more tactful to ignore it?"

"I *feel* green, but I'll be all right when the curtain goes up."

"Good. Well, I must have a word with Mr Dominick, and then get out in front."

"I wish he wasn't here. He makes me far more nervous than Mr Moon."

"He thinks you're really good. He says you carry a good part of the play like the real professional you are."

Drina's pale face suddenly grew rosy.

"Did he really? Then I feel much better!" At that moment she saw Christine, in her Fairy of the Forest costume, standing just behind Miss Whiteway, and was startled by the look of active dislike on Christine's face.

Adele Whiteway turned and saw her, too.

"Good evening, Christine. I hear you're very good."

"Thank you, Miss Whiteway." Christine knew better than to be rude to Mr Dominick's friend and associate, but her face was still unfriendly.

"She only wants me to be ill or something," Drina muttered. "She's my understudy."

"I know," said Adele Whiteway. "And I heard that the understudy rehearsal didn't go off too well. She's good as the Fairy of the Forest, but Mr Dominick said she was far too 'knowing' as Jane. Don't you dare to be ill!"

"I'll try not to be."

"Then the best of luck. I'll be off."

Drina peered through a tiny gap in the heavy red curtains. The members of the orchestra were taking their places and most of the audience seemed to have arrived. The theatre glowed in all the warm beauty of its red and gold, and the attractive little carvings round the Dress Circle caught the light. Looking at it then it was impossible to believe that it would close.

The beginners took their places and Drina reached up to the tree. As the curtain rose, she was supposed to be taking down presents for the soon-to-be departing guests. And then the signals were given, the curtain rose and there was a faint, reassuring buzz of excitement from the audience, which held a large number of children.

The play had begun; it was real, and Drina was immediately lost in it, as though she were really Jane.

And Jan Williams was no longer himself but her slightly troublesome, adventurous brother Charles. Even Queenie was not herself any more, but Sylvia, the older sister, who was so scornful about Charles' idea that it would be nice if Christmas lasted all year.

Drina was happy and assured; not nervous any more. And soon she felt that the audience was with them. Every song and every dance was warmly applauded, and when, as the play progressed, Jane and Charles had won their way through the snowstorm only to find themselves faced with the dangers of the haunted forest, there was a complete, tense silence from beyond the footlights.

The whole play went without a hitch and the audience clearly loved the act in the Land of Christmas. It certainly was colourful and tuneful, full of fun and happiness until Jane and Charles discovered they couldn't go home because the Midnight Witch had extended her power and the way was cut off.

Then, of course, Sylvia and William arrived with the magic star off the Christmas tree that Charles had carelessly dropped and they all set off to brave the terrors of the forest.

At last the play was nearly over. The four were home again in the playroom, being welcomed by their father and mother. Then Drina did her last dance, with the others joining in towards the end, and there was a last song round the Christmas tree, when Jane put the magic star back on the topmost branch.

The curtain came swishing down, and Drina, a little dazed and still rather far away, found Jan winking at her.

"All over! Fun, wasn't it?"

"It was perfect," Drina agreed and they ran forward to join the adult principals in the centre of the front line of bowing performers.

Again and again the curtain rose and they had to sing the final song over again.

As she ran to the dressing-room and wriggled out of the red dress, Drina thought that it was fun to know that they would be doing the play again tomorrow and the day after. Every evening and a few matinées, in fact, until January 14th, except for Christmas Day and Sundays.

"Did you like it?" she asked, when she and her grandparents met.

"Very much," said Mr Chester, who had found the play a refreshing change from too much undiluted ballet. "It's fresh and charming and has some really tuneful music. I didn't know that you could sing so well."

"My voice is so little."

"It carries well, all the same. And Ilonka was delightful in her part."

"She's very pretty, isn't she? And she does dance well. Oh, I'm so tired and *hungry*!"

"We've ordered sandwiches and milk for you at the hotel. And then to bed. You can sleep late in the morning."

Drina tumbled into the taxi and she was still so excited and carried away that the ancient streets and buildings seemed more than ever like a stage set.

Drina was happy until Christmas morning and then, curiously, a feeling of melancholy descended on her. It was a disappointingly grey, cold morning, sleety rather than frosty, and she felt restless and unsettled. Mrs Chester decided that it was too cold for herself or her husband to go out, and Drina set off about eleven to find the others, but changed her mind and climbed onto the city walls.

Up there it was bitterly cold and she seemed to have the whole place almost to herself. She could look down into the practically deserted streets, seeing the cathedral tower rising against the clustered, uneven roofs. Then she came to the part where she could look down on the winding river and see the Welsh hills in the distance.

She stood there in her warm coat and scarf, gazing west and letting her thoughts travel to Grant far away, possibly still asleep in the apartment on Central Park West. He had forgotten her. He had not cared enough even to send a card, and disappointment was all the more because she could tell no one.

People talked a lot of nonsense about the magic of falling in love. It was awful; it upset your life and turned you into a different person, and you couldn't even tell Jenny about it. You couldn't even ask someone for advice on how to forget.

If *only* Grant had sent a card! She had, after some deliberation, sent him one, but, because of a strong streak of pride, she had not posted it until the last possible date for airmail. It wouldn't have been the same thing if Grant had just sent a card because she had reminded him.

Anyway, it was too late now.

She walked right round the walls, a distance of two miles or so, and then went back to the hotel. Ilonka and Jan were coming to have Christmas dinner with them, but they would not arrive for at least half an hour.

Mr and Mrs Chester were both writing letters by a huge fire in the lounge and Drina flung herself down on the rug beside them. Her heart gave a sickening leap when her grandfather put his hand behind him and produced a thick, strong envelope.

"Here you are, Drina," he said, smiling. "I asked the hall porter at the flats to send on any extra mail. It came yesterday. Mostly cards for us, but this for you. I meant to give it to you earlier, but you went out rather quickly. I thought you'd like a surprise from New York on Christmas Day."

"Oh, thank you, Grandfather." Drina took the envelope with a steady hand and kept her tone carefully ordinary. She said, "I'll go up and take my coat off and do my hair."

She asked for her key at the desk and ran up the stairs, not waiting for the lift. Her fingers fumbled with the key and then she was alone in her room with the door shut. She dropped her bag and gloves on the bed and stood staring down at the airmail stamps and at the address written in a firm, clear hand.

When, still rather fumblingly, she got the envelope open a package wrapped in thin, coloured paper fell out. She got that undone and found a neat, paperbacked ballet dictionary, published in New York. Thrust into its pages was a Christmas card and she read the words written in that same firm hand:

To Drina, with best wishes from Grant Rossiter. And then on the opposite side, the message: *I thought you might find this interesting. It may be a little different from a British one. I have not forgotten our pleasant meetings and particularly our trip up the RCA Building. Maybe one day we'll meet again.*

"I have not forgotten our pleasant meetings ... maybe one day we'll meet again."

Drina crossed to the window and stood with the card in her hand, staring unseeingly out into Westgate Street. He had not forgotten! It was Christmas Day and he had not forgotten, after all!

She put the precious card safely into her bag and then

did a wild little dance round the room. Happiness and hope filled her and the earlier mood seemed now to have been silly and unnecessary. Grant was in New York, and maybe still asleep, but he had not forgotten her.

She could not really be angry with her grandfather for holding back the package, for he had thought of it only as a nice little surprise. But she might have been spared some unhappy hours if she had received it sooner.

8

"It's Christine or Me!"

The critics had almost all been kind to *The Land of Christmas* and particularly to Drina. "This charming young dancer, who has shown us, also, that she is an able actress and singer," wrote one critic, who was normally renowned for his caustic comments. Francaster loved the play and the theatre was sold out until the end of the run.

In the foyer the huge book held many hundreds of signatures and there began to be a hope that the theatre might be saved. The local paper carried large headlines:

HOPE FOR THE ROYAL CROWN

ARTS COUNCIL GRANT PROMISED

Townspeople Say "Leave Us Our Theatre"

"But I'm afraid that one can't fight against big business interests," said Mr Chester.

"Oh, Grandfather, don't say that! It's as good as saved. I couldn't bear it if it wasn't. And our play is making a lot of money."

"Well, I may be wrong. I hope so. But I've heard one or two things – oh, well, perhaps they weren't true," said Mr Chester.

The Chesters went back to London and Drina moved into one of the Queen Anne houses, sharing a room with Ilonka, Betty and Meryl. After the Royal Hotel even the nicest of theatrical digs seemed anything but luxury, but Drina cheerfully ate the rather inferior food and queued uncomplainingly for the bathroom. It was fun to be with the others, especially as Queenie and Christine had gone into the other house.

Apart from matinées – and a few extra ones were given as the demand for tickets was so great – they were free in the daytime, and Ilonka, Jan and Drina had great fun together. Together they explored most corners of the old city, gazing with awe at the remains of the great Roman pillars in the cellars of modern shops, and even being shown a Roman central heating system called a hypocaust. Jan began to say that if ever he couldn't be a dancer he would be an archaeologist instead.

The Dominick dancers attracted quite a lot of attention as they walked about Francaster and Drina especially came in for a large amount of notice. Every night when she left the theatre there were crowds at the stage door, all eager for her autograph, and sometimes she had to scrawl "Drina Adams" so often that her wrist ached. But it was fun, and fun to be recognised in the street.

Once or twice she had the urge to write her real name, Andrina Adamo, instead of the more prosaic Drina Adams, but her real name was to be kept for that far-off day – if it ever came – when she was grown up and on her way to being a ballerina. She never used it now because someone might remember that the great Elizabeth Ivory had been, in private life, Mrs Adamo.

On New Year's Eve there was a party on the stage after the show and at midnight Drina could not help remembering that other New Year's Eve, now seeming so long ago, when she had gone to Covent Garden for the first time and learned that her mother had been a great dancer. Soon after that she had been accepted by the Dominick and since then her life had been all dancing. Or so it sometimes seemed. Though of course there were other pleasures. Seeing new places ... meeting new people ... looking at pictures with Ilonka or Rose in the Tate or the National Gallery on Sunday afternoons. So many things.

And now it was another year that might bring all sorts of exciting new experiences. But nothing – oh, nothing so exciting and wonderful as New York, surely?

So the days passed rapidly and pleasantly, with the only real cloud the presence of Queenie and Christine. Though they were next door it was impossible not to see them sometimes during the day, and there they were in the dressing-room at night, giggling together and saying unkind and catty things about both Ilonka and Drina.

"Christine has the tongue of an–an asp!" Drina said savagely one evening. "I hate her!"

"Me, I won't waste my energy on hating her," Ilonka said loftily.

"I don't know. You once said you could murder her. She gets under my skin and she knows it," Drina groaned. "I wish she'd sprain an ankle or something and keep out of our way for a while."

But Christine continued in apparently abounding health and her tongue was at it every opportunity it got.

Drina enjoyed exploring with Ilonka and Jan. Often she went to the cathedral, where she was constantly finding something new – or rather, very old – to fascinate her and remind her of the days when the monks worked and prayed and slept in the Benedictine abbey.

In winter the cathedral closed at dusk and several times Drina was the last to leave. It was sheltered in the cloister garth, so quiet and beautiful with its fishpond and little bare trees, and she often perched on a seat for a while, looking round at the rose-red walls and the stained glass windows of the surrounding cloisters.

It was a good place for thinking and dreaming; a great contrast to the busy city and the exciting working hours in the theatre.

One afternoon as she stepped out into the cloisters she heard voices and saw two girls in the distance, standing on a corner of the cloisters, where there was a door into the church.

Queenie and Christine! Now what, thought Drina indignantly, were *they* doing in the cathedral? It was unreasonable, but she was almost beginning to think of it as her own private place, and her enemies were not the kind of people to enjoy the peace and intense silence of the ancient building.

Christine and Queenie had, in fact, followed her there, curious to know where she slipped away to. But Drina did not know this and thought that they were there by accident.

She turned smartly in the opposite direction and went to peep into the great refectory, where the thirteenth-century reader's pulpit was still as perfect as it had been centuries ago. Here a monk had read aloud while the others dined and she had often tried to picture them at the long, bare tables.

She was also very fond of the Norman cellarium, which, with its thick pillars and low arches, seemed the most ancient part of the whole building. It was not always open, as it was used as a sort of storeroom, but that afternoon she found the door half-open and slipped in.

"But I mustn't be long," she told herself. "It's beginning to get dark. I don't want to spend the night here."

All the same, she took a few steps into the dimness. It was far warmer in there than in the draughty stone cloisters, and there was the stuffy smell of coke-fumes. Drina stood with her chilly hands held out to a warm iron stove and thought how strange it was to be in Francaster, about which she had scarcely heard until she had been invited to act there. In three days the play would close and that would be very sad, as such a thing always was. Then back to London and Rose, and soon the new term at the Dominick.

The slamming of the heavy door startled her, and for a moment she hardly realised what had happened. Then she darted forward and wrenched at the thick iron handle. The door wouldn't move.

It seemed, suddenly, to be much darker, and there wasn't a sound anywhere but for the faint rustling of the burning coke in the stove. Someone must have shut the door and locked it, not knowing that she was there.

She began to call in a rather panic-stricken way, not at all sure that her voice would be heard through the thick walls and the stout oak door. Possibly the same door that had been there when the monks used the place.

The door did not open, and suddenly, the memory of Queenie and Christine came to her. There had been a huge key in the lock. She remembered it now, and maybe they had seen her enter and had had the sudden plan of making her a prisoner. With her safely out of the way Christine would play Jane …

"Oh, how silly!" Drina said aloud. "That would be like a bad book. They just wouldn't."

But commonsense told her that Christine would.

Drina began to move cautiously forward, taking care not to fall over anything. The dimness and the silence were now definitely menacing and she was haunted by the thought of having to spend the night there. She would be warm enough, but it would be an uncomfortable resting-place. Besides, there was the play.

Once, in Edinburgh, she had missed a performance through no fault of her own. It had been a nightmare experience and she had no wish to repeat it. Get out somehow she must!

She edged her way round the Norman pillars and found herself in a sort of alcove, where there was a great pile of coke. Here it was lighter and she looked up in wild relief to see a sort of open hatch and, beyond it, a stone passage.

Scrambling and slithering she got on top of the coke and managed to heave herself halfway through the hatch. As she was turning to let herself down on the other side a bell began to clang through the building. The cathedral was closing!

The passage was one that she hadn't been in before, but she turned right and by great good luck soon found herself by a side door that led out into Cathedral Square. She dashed out into the open air and up the steps. It was much lighter outside, but the lamps were already alight, and ahead, just walking under the great arch of the Cathedral Gate, were Queenie and Christine. They seemed to be arguing, and, as she drew nearer, their heated voices reached Drina.

"We shouldn't have done it!" Queenie was saying fiercely. "Someone will find her, anyway. They must

have a pretty good look to see that no one's left inside."

"Oh, rubbish! It was a golden opportunity. She played right into our hands. Besides, who's going to look into that cellar, or whatever it was? No, she's stuck there and I'll get my chance. Jane's a much bigger part than the Fairy of the Forest."

Drina was wearing rubber-soled shoes and she was upon them, on the far side of the gate, before they realised her presence. Her easily roused temper was at fever-heat and she clutched Christine's arm so fiercely that Christine gave a startled yelp.

"I'm out, you see! How *could* you be so wicked? How *dare* you do such a thing."

Christine stood stock-still, her eyes wide.

"How could I do what? You can't be well, Drina."

"I'm well, but so mad I could – could hit you in full sight of everyone in Northgate Street! You've gone too far this time and I've a good mind to go straight to someone in authority."

"You'd never dare," said Christine uneasily, giving up the pretence of not knowing what she was talking about. "Besides, you can't prove anything."

"Maybe not, but I'd have a really good try."

"It was just for fun," Queenie said. "And dear little Drina got frightened."

"Fun! It's not my idea of a joke!" And Drina stormed away and presently hurled herself into the bedroom she shared with the others. They were all there, writing letters home.

They stared in amazement as Drina burst in.

"What on earth's the matter, Drina? Why! You're filthy!"

"Small wonder. I've been mountaineering over coke." And Drina poured out the story. "I *won't* tell anyone, of course. But I wish Christine were at the bottom of the sea. It's her or me – I'm sure it is. We can't *both* stay at the Dominick!"

"Oh, Drina! But she'll never leave."

"She may overstep the mark one day, though," Betty said.

"Not she. She's to clever to do anything that people in authority may pounce on. I'm going to have a bath." And Drina flung off her coat and began to unfasten her dress.

"The water's stone cold."

"Oh, bother!" For a moment Drina bitterly missed the unending hot water at the Royal Hotel.

She washed as best she could and was calmer by the time they were ready to leave for the theatre. But now she knew, if she had not known long before really, that it was war between herself and Christine.

During the last days of the play Drina looked with increasing affection at the Royal Crown Theatre, and she never doubted that it was safe enough now. The lease had not yet been renewed, but it surely would be, with the townspeople *and* the Arts Council behind the project.

It was therefore an immense shock when, with Ilonka and Jan, she entered the stage door for the last performance to be met by the glum face of the old stage doorman.

"Well, the old place has had it."

"Had it? But – but it can't have!"

"Haven't you seen the local paper?"

"Why, no."

"It's all in there. The owners have accepted a right big offer and the theatre is to be pulled down in the spring."

"But they *can't*!" Drina cried despairingly.

"Believe me, they can. Money talks nowadays. What's a theatre compared to shops and offices? And I've been here for thirty years, that I have."

"But perhaps the paper is wrong," Jan said reasonably. "Journalists do get hold of the wrong story sometimes."

"No, it's true enough. I was having a word with the manager just now."

By the time the curtain rose, everyone in the cast knew that the theatre was doomed and that the red curtain would never rise again on any show. Perhaps because of this they seemed to put their very hearts into the play and it went better than ever before.

The audience clapped every item and cheered at the end of each act and Drina was filled with a heady excitement that for a time overshadowed her sorrow. Oh, there could be nothing so thrilling and satisfying in the whole world as being on stage in the glare of the lights, knowing that a whole audience was with you!

But the end of the play drew near at last. They were back in the playroom, Drina had danced, and they were gathering for the last song. The tree sparkled above them and outside the window the snow was falling.

Down swished the curtain and suddenly Drina's mood of elation was gone. As the curtain rose again and she looked out into the dim auditorium and heard the cheers and the eager clapping her eyes were wet. It was over, but it wouldn't have been so sad if another play had been opening soon. As it was …

Curtain after curtain. The house-lights were up now and the audience was standing but still clapping. The whole cast waved and smiled, but other eyes than Drina's were over-bright.

Now the curtain was down and it was time to go. In the morning they would leave Fancaster and the weeks there would soon seem like a dream. Everyday life at the Dominick would claim the Londoners again.

BOOK TWO
Ballet in France

1

Invitation to Paris

The spring term seemed long and hard. The weather was continuously bad and many dancers were away with colds. Drina survived until the beginning of March and then developed such a bad cold on her chest that school was out of the question.

She gave in, at first with a show of reluctance, but secretly she was most unusually relieved. Never before had she been glad not to have to go to the Dominick, but she had been finding life there a strain, and it was, in many ways, a great relief to lie in bed for a couple of days, playing records and reading.

"I've never known you to be so good," Mrs Chester remarked, much puzzled even though she was relieved. "Do you feel *very* ill?"

"Oh, no, thank you, Granny. I'm just tired, that's all."

"Tired? Well, I'm not surprised after all the hard work you've been doing. They do seem to be driving you now. And the weather has been shocking enough to depress anyone."

Well, it was true that she had been working desperately hard both at her dancing and her school work, and there were so many other things as well, including her piano lessons and her outside interests. But, though all these things, and the dreary winter weather, might have contributed to Drina's sudden weariness, they were by no means the whole reason. It was rather that there was something deep in her that was not quite right.

She had never completely regained her pleasure in being at the Dominick and this, apart from the fact that she had not stopped thinking of Grant Rossiter, was mostly due to Christine Gifford. To Christine *and* Queenie, but Queenie – once so trying in herself – was now only a pale shadow of the much more unpleasant Christine.

Ever since the beginning of term Christine had set herself to make Drina's life as unbearable as possible and she had an uncanny way of putting her finger on the things that hurt. Drina had, for the most part, ignored her, but it was dreadful to spend most of each day in the company of so nasty an enemy. She could not escape Christine, from the morning ballet class to the end of the afternoon. During ordinary lessons Christine sat fairly near to her and had a disconcerting habit of staring across and muttering remarks to Queenie whenever Drina had to speak or read aloud or even take up her book to be marked.

It was surprising just how deeply Christine had managed to get under Drina's skin and she evidently sensed her power.

I hate myself for being so silly, Drina confessed to Rose in a letter. *I could just about put up with her at Chalk Green, though I was really glad when she was moved into another dormitory, but now – oh, Rose, nothing seems fun any more. I'd wish that you were here, except that you hate Christine even more than I do. Even London doesn't seem such fun any more, but that's probably because the weather has been so foul. Sometimes I wonder if spring will ever come?*

So now, a few days after writing the letter to Rose, Drina lay in bed and coughed and sneezed, while the sleet beat against the windows.

Mrs Chester, privately rather disturbed, poured out her worries to her husband that evening.

"She doesn't seem quite herself. In fact, I've thought so for months and it's got worse. Do you think she's worrying about anything in particular?"

"I shouldn't think so. They seem satisfied enough with her progress at the Dominick and she had a great success in the Christmas play. After all, fifteen is an awkward age. She's matured a lot –"

"Well, in some ways, but she's still very small for her age and so pale just now. But I asked the doctor and he says there's nothing really the matter with her beyond the bad cold. He said she'd pick up when the weather gets better."

"*When* it does," said Mr Chester, with a sigh. He had been thinking a good deal about the pleasures of wintering in a drier, warmer climate.

Drina was away from school for a week and when she returned Christine was away ill, which was a great relief. On Saturday afternoon Drina, Ilonka and Jan Williams went to the Royal Opera House and *that* was pleasant, too. Drina was always happy to go to Covent Garden and she deeply enjoyed *Mam'zelle Angot, La Fête Etrange* and *Le Baiser de la Fée*.

Then, suddenly, the seemingly unending winter did show signs of giving place to spring. The trees in the parks were in bud and suddenly some of them were covered with a faint green haze. The air was warmer, though it was still often wet, and one afternoon after school Drina and Ilonka walked through St James's Park and found a magnolia in full flower. The waxy blossoms glowed pearly white through the gentle haze of rain and there was a smell of grass and earth.

Drina lifted her face and sniffed ecstatically.

"I can *smell* the spring now, and about time, too! Oh, Ilonka, I feel as though I'm coming alive again!"

"Me also," Ilonka agreed, with a little skip that landed her in a puddle. "And soon it will be holidays."

"Not until April 14th. This is such a long term, with Easter being so late." But everything did suddenly seem more hopeful and, even with Christine back at the Dominick, Drina tackled school work and dancing with renewed enthusiasm.

She was rather startled a week or two before the end of term to be sent for by Miss Volonaise.

"What can it be for?" she asked Ilonka.

"Something nice," Ilonka answered hopefully.

"Well, I don't know. I'd better go and see." And she set off up the stairs to Miss Volonaise's office. As on that previous occasion when she had been invited to go to Francaster, Mr Dominick was there, too, sitting on the windowsill.

He turned and grinned at her, and Drina could not resist grinning back. She was still somewhat in awe of Mr Dominick, but he had a disconcerting way of treating her as an equal, at least when they were alone.

"And how are *you*? I haven't spoken to you for a long time."

"Very well, thank you, Mr Dominick."

"She had a bad cold and she still looks pale, but I fancy she's all right," said Miss Volonaise, surprising Drina, who was still humble enough not to expect her absence of nearly a month before to be noticed by anyone so important.

"Well, what you need is a change. A change of air and a change of scene. You know that the Company is going to Paris for the last week in April and the first week in

May?"

Drina's heart leaped. Had they invited her there to tell her that?

"Oh, yes. Terza was telling Ilonka and me all about it. She loves Paris. She's so thrilled."

"And do you love it, too?"

"I – oh, I've never been. Or only just when I was on my way back from Italy. I just saw the Sacré-Coeur on La Butte de Montmartre. From the train, you know."

"What? Never seen Paris in the spring? The chestnuts in flower and all the rest?"

"Never, Mr Dominick." He was teasing her, but could there be any reason for the questions? The head of the School and Company wouldn't invite her there just to talk about the Paris trees in flower.

"We'll have to rectify that. We were rather thinking of taking you with us."

Drina's pale cheeks suddenly flamed and her heart was thumping hard. She couldn't speak.

Smiling, Marianne Volonaise began to explain.

"We're reviving the production of *Casse Noisette* that we took to the Edinburgh Festival last year. We had intended to give Marcia Merrander the rôle of Little Clara." Marcia Merrander was one of the youngest members of the *corps de ballet*; a pretty, childish-looking girl of barely seventeen.

Drina stood looking at them in silence and Miss Volonaise went on:

"This morning in her ballet class she somehow pulled a muscle very badly. Rather as you did some time ago, when you couldn't dance for some weeks. So that, I'm afraid, makes it impossible for her to go to Paris. There is no one else really suitable, so we thought we'd take you, with Rose Conway understudying you, as in Edinburgh."

"Oh, Miss Volonaise!" Drina brought her hands together so sharply that they gave a loud clap. She blushed again, this time with embarrassment. "Oh, how wonderful! Oh, I've *longed* to go to Paris, especially to see Montmartre."

The two adults exchanged glances. When Elizabeth Ivory's daughter was happy and animated her face was utterly alive and bore a strong resemblance, in spite of the difference in colouring, to the great dancer who had also had such a vivid personality.

"We're glad you're so pleased," Mr Dominick said. "By the way, Igor will be going, too."

"Igor?" Drina had not seen much of Igor that term. He had begun to seem almost grown up and had been about more with the older male students.

"Yes. He's going to have the rôle of Franz."

"Oh!" Drina's face broke into a smile. Franz was Little Clara's rather unpleasant brother, who broke the Nutcracker Doll.

"He wasn't keen at first. Feels himself too old, we think. But now he's agreed. By the way," Mr Dominick went on, "I telephoned Adele Whiteway just now. She's going along with the Company and she says she'll be delighted to have you and Rose with her. So your grandmother needn't worry at all."

"Oh, how splendid!"

"I'll telephone your grandmother, too. She won't be best pleased, but I'm afraid she must get used to the idea that you are bound to travel."

Drina escaped from the office with burning cheeks and in a state of wild excitement. She was so thrilled that she forgot discretion. It was the mid-afternoon break and most of her class were gathered in the corridor, since the day was, once again, wet.

"Oh, Ilonka! Imagine it! Rose and I are going to Paris

with the Company after Easter. They're taking *Casse Noisette* and Marcia Merrander has pulled a muscle, so –''

"Well, really!" Queenie said indignantly. Drina had not noticed that she and Christine were so near.

"So little Drina is the favourite again!" Christine chipped in, her face ugly with jealousy and spite.

Abruptly aware of what the others might all think Drina said defensively:

"It isn't favouritism. You know that really. I was Little Clara before, and I took the part, so now that Marcia –"

"*You* get everything!" Christine said savagely. "You go to the Edinburgh Festival, you get the best part in the Christmas play, and now Paris. If only I had the courage I'd go to Miss Volonaise right now and tell her what I think of it and *her*. She and Mr Dominick don't think of the rest of us. It's my belief that there's some *reason* for favouring Drina Adams."

Drina was dead white, for once more, probably unknowingly, Christine had put her finger on a sore point. She was never quite convinced that the great ones were not influenced by the fact that Ivory was her mother. She had not noticed, and neither had Christine, that the others had grown uneasily silent and were trying to signal to them.

"It isn't true! Rose is going, too. It's just that we're the most suitable –"

"Perhaps you went and *asked*. You've got cheek enough for anything."

"I *didn't*. Of *course* I didn't. It was a complete surprise."

"Well, I think that Madam –"

"Your opinion, of course, is very interesting, Christine," said a cool voice, and there was Miss Volonaise herself, standing only a few feet away.

The crowd began to melt away and Christine shrank until she looked nothing but a frightend, embarrassed fifteen-year-old girl. Drina, appalled, leaned against the wall for support.

"I – I didn't mean – I was only j-joking. Madam –"

Marianne Volonaise looked at her long and coldly.

"I'll see you in my office at once. There's the bell. You run back to your class, Drina."

The rest of the afternoon was really terrible. Christine did not show herself again and a girl who had been sent out to wash her hands reported in whispers that her things had gone from the cloakroom. Queenie sat at her desk looking white and alarmed, and looked even worse after an interview with Miss Volonaise and the headmistress, Miss Lane. But none of her class could question her immediately, because she returned some minutes before the end of afternoon school.

Drina felt sick and frightened. She hated Christine and had longed for her to leave the Dominick, but it was dreadful to feel that the trouble was somehow *her* fault. Also, Christine's words rankled bitterly. Every atom of pleasure in the proposed visit to Paris had quite gone. She was not in the least comforted by the fact that, when they were at last free from lessons, public opinion seemed to be entirely on her side.

"Christine's been asking for it for years," Meryl said sensibly. "I've heard tales about the things she said and did at Chalk Green. Stop looking half-dead, Drina, do!"

"I *feel* half-dead," Drina said shakily.

"Why should *you* worry? Christine wished you nothing but ill. Queenie was the only one who liked her."

"Queenie will hate me more than ever now. Do you think that Christine really has gone?"

"Gone and good riddance to her," said Betty roundly.

But no one knew for certain until they could ask the sombre-faced Queenie. Queenie had been kept back by their teacher and only appeared when most people were ready to leave.

"Yes," said Queenie, unusually subdued. "She's gone and she isn't coming back."

"But what did Miss Volonaise and Miss Lane say to *you*?"

"They told me not to discuss it," said Queenie, and marched off alone, her shoulders hunched. But not before she had cast a look of acute dislike at Drina.

Drina could bear it no longer. She said to Ilonka:

"Don't wait for me. I've got to find Miss Volonaise."

"But, Drina, you can't!" She hasn't sent for you. People just don't go looking for Madam. Besides, she may be busy."

"I *must* see her. I shall tell her that I won't go to Paris."

Miss Volonaise was not in her office, but appeared in the corridor as Drina was lingering there. She put out a firm hand and drew Drina into the office.

"I'm glad you're here. I had meant to try and catch you, but it's quite a business – expelling someone within the space of an hour. *Not* a thing we make a habit of." Then she added quickly, "Don't look so tragic, Drina. It was none of it your fault."

"But it must have been. Somehow I made Christine hate me."

"You were not the only one Christine hated, by all accounts. This was just the culminating thing, following on some trouble we had last week. She had been bullying one of the youngest juniors. She came here from Chalk Green with a very bad report indeed and we were most reluctant to keep her on, even though her dancing was so good. But we decided to give her another chance, and then last week – this is in the strictest confidence, of course. Now, Drina, listen to me."

"Yes, Madam." Drina looked up at her almost shrinkingly. In spite of the way Miss Volonaise had spoken to her – almost as though she were a fellow adult – she suddenly felt that there was a vast, yawning gulf between them. Well, of course there was. Drina Adams and the great Marianne Volonaise.

"You are a little idiot!" said Miss Volonaise, suddenly and surprisingly, smiling with astonishing warmth. "A fathead! Do you hear me?"

"Y-yes, Madam." But tears were nearer than smiles.

"I am not used to being disbelieved, and I tell you this for the last time. You have always been chosen on your merits and not – repeat not – because your mother was Elizabeth Ivory, which, in any case, we didn't know until the end of the Edinburgh Festival last year. You are a promising dancer and the only other way you are perhaps a little different from most of your contemporaries is that we tend to talk to you more freely. I suppose that *is* because of your mother, to some extent, but it's also because you are a sensible person and have great character. Show some of that character now, please. Come to Paris, be happy, and forget this whole unpleasant business."

Drina was now crying openly.

"I'm so s-sorry. It was all so h-horrible. And – and I was going to tell you I c-couldn't go to Paris."

"You are going, and you're to telephone Rose tonight and have a long talk with her. You may reverse the charge to Chalk Green Manor. I'll let Miss Sutherland know. You are to make cheerful plans and you are both to look forward to seeing Montmartre. You may tell

Rose about Christine, but she is not to discuss it with the others. In the morning Miss Lane is going to make a brief announcement about Christine to the whole school and then that is to be the end of the matter."

"Y – yes, Madam. But what will happen to Christine?"

Miss Volonaise raised her eyebrows.

"She told us very defiantly that she will go to a Stage School. One of them may take her, as she has talent. I don't think that you need worry about Christine's future." She put her arm round the slender, shaking shoulders and Drina had no idea of the warm feeling that was in her heart for this dark, sensitive girl who at times found life so difficult.

"Now dry your eyes and go home. Or go and see Adele Whiteway. You're fond of her, aren't you?"

"Yes. She makes me feel – more sensible."

"All right. Hop off there. She told me she was working at home this afternoon."

Drina obeyed, for she did not want to go home until she was more composed. And Adele Whiteway, already warned by telephone, received her with her usual warm kindness, plied her with tea and chocolate biscuits and allowed her to tell the tale.

Then she said briskly:

"Yes. Well, this has been boiling up for a long time. I heard about last week's trouble, though it was kept from the school. You need have no feeling of guilt at all. Now let's talk about Paris and forget Christine. You and Rose will have a wonderful time."

"Rose will be so thrilled. She's never been abroad."

"You'll be able to take her about. I expect you'll buy a street map, as you always do, and you speak French quite well, don't you? We'll all go to a good, quite cheap hotel that I know by the Gare du Nord. The theatre where you'll be dancing is down by the Seine, near the Place du Châtelet, but you can easily travel on the Métro, and the hotel will be nice and convenient for Montmartre."

"*Oh*! That will be lovely!"

So when Drina went home at last she was almost her usual self and was able to talk with enthusiasm about Paris. Mrs Chester, of course, was not very pleased, but she did not object.

"So long as Miss Whiteway is with you both you'll be all right."

When Drina spoke to Rose, her friend already knew about the Paris trip and was almost incoherent with excitement.

"Drina, I can't believe it! What will Dad and Mum say?"

"They'll let you go, surely?"

"Oh, of course. They wouldn't stand in my way, but they do have rather funny ideas about foreigners," Rose said tolerantly. She had met so many students of different nationalities at the Dominick and Chalk Green that her own experience was considerably wider than that of her parents.

Then Drina told her rapidly about the Christine affair, adding Miss Volonaise's warning that it was not to be talked about, and Rose said:

"How horrible for you! But I'm glad she's gone and you must be, too. Life will be ten times easier."

"There's still Queenie, but she seems very subdued."

"Well, she may be. She's not been so much better than Christine and I bet that Miss Volonaise knows it. It's my belief that they know everything."

"You thought once that they didn't know we existed."

"That was when I was young and innocent. Now I

see that they've got their fingers firmly on things. Oh, Drina, Paris!"

"Oh, Rose, Paris!" Drina repeated, and soon afterwards she spread all her Utrillo postcards out on her bed. It seemed amazing that soon she would walk those little cobbled streets in reality, that she would see those quiet little squares in the spring.

And not only Montmartre. There would be the whole of Paris; the chestnut trees in the Champs-Elysées ... the Cathedral of Notre Dame on its island ... the smart shops in the Rue de la Paix ... the Tuileries Gardens and the Luxembourg Gardens ... the Musée National d'Art Moderne that held so many of the paintings she longed to see.

Paris in the spring, and with Rose. Next to going back to New York it was the nicest thing that could have happened.

2
Morning in Montmartre

Jenny came to London for three nights over Easter. For some months now they had written few letters, and had only had a few unsatisfactory telephone conversations. Drina looked forward to her visit with more anxiety than pleasure, but she had little time for thinking, as rehearsals for *Casse Noisette* had started almost at once, and then – with school finished – she was also busy reading up Paris and planning what clothes she would take with her.

Renée Randall was to dance the Sugar Plum Fairy, with Peter Bernoise as the Nutcracker Prince, and it was sad to rehearse with the Dominick and know that there was no chance of seeing Catherine Colby. But everyone welcomed Drina and Rose warmly and the rehearsals were fun, if also extremely hard work.

At the suggestion of Mr Dominick and the company ballet mistress, Rose was to dance Little Clara at one matinée and one evening performance. Rose was thrilled but apologetic, until she was sure that Drina did not mind.

"Of course I don't mind, silly. You ought to have a

chance. Understudying is really deadly, I should think."

"But you're the well-known one."

"Rubbish! And, besides, you're far prettier than me."

Rose blushed.

"Me pretty?"

"Lovely. Didn't you know?"

"No, I didn't. And you – why, you're striking. You *look* like a dancer."

"Mutual admiration society, this is," Drina said lightly, and changed the subject.

She met Jenny at Paddington on the Saturday, feeling stiff and shy, as well as uneasy. And her feelings did not alter when Jenny appeared, looking so tall and grown-up. She was almost sixteen now, but looked far older. She talked easily enough, but both were aware of constraint as the taxi carried them towards Westminster.

How different it had been in the old days, when they met each other again. Drina felt sad and almost desperate, but there seemed little she could do or say.

Mrs Chester, who had not seen Jenny for a long time, was privately very shocked. The pretty little plump girl with fair hair seemed a world away from this rather hard young woman with unhappy eyes. She found it almost impossible to remember that Jenny was only a few months older than Drina. For all her experiences of new places and people, in spite of mild fame and undoubted professionalism, Drina seemed to her still a child, while Jenny emphatically did not.

That evening Jenny and Drina strolled in St James's Park, amidst all the beauty of April, but Jenny did not seem moved by it. She talked about the farm a little, but mainly about the Grossdale Comprehensive. Some things she liked, but she would be glad to leave in the summer, even though it meant working in the office run by a friend of her father's.

"I'm lucky to be certain of a job," she said, in the hard tone she had used most of the time. "The money will be quite good, so I can help out at home."

"Oh, but Jenny ..." Drina began, remembering all Jenny's hopes and plans of going to an agricultural college. But her friend froze her with a look. Her father's bankruptcy had changed all that.

Some of her remarks and comments, even her language, made Drina open her eyes in surprise and even wince once or twice, and Jenny noticed it.

"What a baby you still are!" she said, laughing, but not in the warm and friendly manner of old. "I believe you're shocked!"

"Oh, Jenny, no," Drina said hastily. "But isn't it – not very nice to talk like that?"

She could have bitten her tongue out a moment later, for Jenny immediately looked angry.

"Maybe it is. I don't know or care. All the others talk like that. Far worse, really. I'm with them now, so I may as well conform. After all, you aren't really a baby. You've been about and seen things and met far more people than I have."

"I know. Yes, of course." And Drina naturally had no words with which to express her dislike of Jenny's new manner and conversation. She was neither ignorant nor particularly innocent, and it was true that she had "been about", but something about Jenny now made her very unhappy.

It was not really a satisfactory weekend, but Jenny did gradually soften and become more her old self. On the last night, with a freshly washed face and surprisingly childish pyjamas – blue and white – she seemed almost the old Jenny. They sat in Drina's room and suddenly

Jenny burst out:

"I *know* I've been awful! But that dreadful hard shell is beginning to hem me in. Oh, Drina, don't let it! If I lose *you* then all my old life has gone. Don't drift away."

And Drina, very moved, said shakily:

"I won't. I do understand."

"I wonder if you do? Lucky you, you've got everything. And most of all you have hope for the future. I haven't deviated a scrap; I still only want farming and the country. But I shan't get them. I have to earn as soon as I can. I *know* what's happening to me, but I can't stop it. Only don't hate me or despise me. For I can't bear it."

"Jenny, I don't. I – I admire you very much. If – if I were in your position I couldn't face it."

"You would. You'd have to, but you might turn into a different person. But nothing awful will happen to *you*. You'll be a great dancer, and just now you're going to Paris. Lucky you and equally lucky Rose!"

"Rose is poor and has no nice clothes. She isn't all that lucky."

"She's got the Dominick and her talent and you. I call that lucky. Still, I won't moan any more, so long as you understand."

So, in the end, it was with deep regret that Drina waved goodbye to Jenny, but once more there was little time for thinking, for she was off to Paris in a very short time.

It was true what she had said about Rose, and Rose was finding the question of clothes for Paris a great problem, even though her mother had hastily made her two pretty dresses.

The last London rehearsal went off very well, and when they all assembled again it would be in the Paris theatre.

Young Igor Dominick had been very friendly towards Drina and Rose and seemed to assume that they would see a good deal of each other in Paris. He had entertained them with accounts of the places they must see, but Drina, at least, was not very forthcoming.

"I can't forget the way he treated us in Edinburgh," she said to Rose, as they walked part of the way home after the rehearsal. "And in Paris he'll have his Cousin Marie again, I suppose. I'm not going to be dropped like a hot potato when she appears. Monsieur Igor can do as he pleases, but he can count me out from the very start."

"He's puzzled because you aren't warmer towards him," said Rose, grinning.

"He can puzzle. I *like* Igor – or I did until Edinburgh – but I don't trust him. He's far too pleased with himself."

"He's very handsome."

"Of course, but it isn't enough," Drina said coolly. "I – I want kindness and – and consistency in my friends."

"You won't get either from Igor, but he is fun."

"Then you can have him. He seems rather struck on you anyhow."

Rose laughed and let the matter go.

On Drina's last evening at home her grandmother said anxiously:

"Miss Whiteway is very sensible but she won't look after you as I try to do. So do take care, mind the traffic, and I hope you have a good time."

"I will take care, Granny. There's no need at all to worry."

Though she *had* been abroad, Mrs Chester would have found that her own views on French people, particularly French men, coincided to some extent with Mr and Mrs Conway's. But she said no more. Drina had commonsense and she could no longer be protected like a child.

The next morning Drina was ready in plenty of time and her two neat little pale green suitcases stood in the hall. The Dominick Company was flying to Paris *en masse*, but Miss Whiteway, who knew Mrs Chester's views on flying, had booked seats on the Rome Express. This was the train on which Drina had returned from Genoa, and it seemed much more than a year ago.

"Then I *was* a child," Drina thought, as the taxi carried her towards Victoria. "Now I'm not."

She had tactfully refused her grandmother's offer to see them off, and Rose was waiting by the main bookstall when Drina arrived. Rose was pinker than usual and seemed very excited.

"Oh, Drina, I've so often slipped in here to watch people going abroad, and now I'm going myself! I just can't believe that we'll be in Paris this evening!"

"It is very exciting," Drina admitted.

"I've been looking at labels. People going to Rome and Naples and all sorts of other places. But Paris is enough for me."

Miss Whiteway arrived then, and soon they had taken their seats on the train. Rose watched everyone with wide bright eyes and gave a gasp of relief and satisfaction as the whistles blew and the long train slid slowly out of the station.

"I really thought that something might stop me going at the very last minute."

Though she had once been to Switzerland as well as Italy, Drina, too, was very thrilled with the journey. The day was the warmest there had been so far that spring and the Channel crossing was perfect, the water calm and blue and the air so clear that France was visible after a very short time.

Rose gazed towards the unknown country with

wistful excitement.

"France! Just think! And to *dance* there. That makes it ten times more exciting. We're not just tourists. It will make us belong a little."

They followed Miss Whiteway to the express at Calais, picking their way through piles of luggage, excited blue-clad porters and anxious English people. Miss Whiteway spoke French fluently and there were no difficulties. Soon after the train had left Calais an attendant came along the corridor ringing a bell and it was time for a late lunch.

The dining-car was cool and shady and Rose stared at the tables with incredulous delight.

"You can *tell* it's another country. Look at the rolls and the bottles of wine! Oh, I *wish* we could have wine!"

"I daresay you can have just a little," Adele Whiteway said indulgently. "But don't blame me if you sleep all afternoon. I'll have a bottle and share it with you."

Drina and Rose were very hungry and made short work of the delicious *hors d'oeuvres*, veal and salad and French fried potatoes. They finished with ices and coffee, but never forgot to stare out of the windows, at the French countryside bathing in the first hot sun of the year.

The chalky fields were crossed by white paths, very sharply etched in the bright light, and the little villages they flashed through might, with their pale colour-washed buildings, bright awnings and café tables, have been in Italy.

Presently they were flashing through the most beautiful woodland and Drina sighed contentedly.

"It's wonderful country! I thought before that it was a little like the Chilterns."

"It's *France*," said Rose. "But I see what you mean."

Then, very soon after six o'clock, they approached Paris, and grey buildings crowded on either side of the railway track. Drina, wildly excited by this time, pointed out the white domes of the Sacré-Coeur on La Butte de Montmartre, but a glimpse was all they had, because the train drew up in the Gare du Nord and Miss Whiteway secured a porter, gave a few rapid instructions and bustled them away.

"The hotel is only across the street. Very convenient, you see, though it's not a particularly attractive part. Don't get lost, Rose. You look very far away."

Rose obediently clutched Drina's arm and gasped as they left the great station and came out into the noise and glare of the wide streets.

"*Remember* which side of the road the traffic is on," said Adele Whiteway. "I don't want two dead dancers on my hands."

"Oh, I *wish* I'd worked harder at French!" Rose cried, as they paused halfway across the road, with the traffic whirling along on either side. "But it wouldn't have done a bit of good. People speak so fast. Did you hear those porters in the station? And that excited party who seemed in trouble?"

"They were only meeting someone," said Drina.

"Good gracious! I thought they'd lost their luggage and half a dozen children! Dad said the French were excitable. I've never seen them *en masse* before."

The entrance hall of the hotel seemed dark after the sunlight, but their welcome was warm and they were led quickly to the lift. Their rooms were three single ones, side by side, and amazingly quiet because they faced a sort of deep court.

Rose wandered from one room to the other, sniffing the air.

"Even the polish they use is different! Oh, what shall

we do now? May we go and see the river and the
theatre and Notre Dame and –?''

"Now, look!" said Adele Whiteway. "You've had a
long, exciting day and you're going to bed very early.
Unpack some of your things and then we're going
round the corner to a little restaurant I know. No
exploring tonight, but if you wake up early you can go
and see Montmatre or do what you like. Have breakfast
up there if you want to. You don't have to be at the
theatre until eleven. I trust you both to be sensible, and
do watch the traffic. But if Drina didn't get run over in
Milan or New York surely she won't here?''

"It always takes a day or two to get used to it," said
Drina.

So they unpacked and then set off round the corner
through the strolling evening crowds.

"It might be somewhere around the Euston Road,"
said Drina.

But Rose was shocked.

"It's Paris!"

"I know. But it's not unlike. Only more cheerful, with
people eating out on the pavements.''

"It really isn't a very attractive part, but Drina will like
it because of Montmartre," said Adele Whiteway. "And
the hotel's good. My little restaurant is good, too, and
very cheap. You can go anywhere you want to by
Métro.''

The two girls were impressed by the welcome Miss
Whiteway received at the small restaurant, which was
run by an Italian family. They managed to get a table
outside, sheltered from the passers-by by a painted
fence and little trees in blue tubs. Drina distinguished
herself by speaking to the waiter in Italian, which
delighted him, and they ate very light omelettes and
salads as they watched the passing crowds. The street

was shadowy, but the sky was blue overhead and it was surprisingly warm.

"Lovely summer at last!" said Drina contentedly. "How wonderful it is after so much horrible cold."

"It's only the end of April."

"Still, it feels warm like summer. Oh, I *wish* we could go and walk along the Champs-Elysées!" She ended the remark with a stifled yawn, which was almost at once echoed by Rose, and Miss Whiteway laughed.

"Bed for both of you. And Montmartre in the morning, if you're awake early. That's the best time to go. You'll love it."

"I'm almost frightened," Drina confessed. "I've pictured it for so long as a sort of remote little enchanted village above Paris –"

"I hope you find it so. I do, except at the height of the season. You're seeing it at the very best time."

So Drina and Rose went obediently to bed and both fell asleep almost at once. It was six o'clock and the sun was already shining brightly when Drina awoke. She immediately tumbled into the corridor and knocked softly on Rose's door.

"Wake up! I'm getting dressed."

They set off through the broad grey streets that seemed washed and clean in the early light. There were plenty of people about already, but it looked very different from the heat and noise of evening. Rose was timid and much admired Drina for the calm way she set off up the Boulevard de Magenta.

"Are you sure this is the right way?"

"Quite sure. I've learned this part of the street map off by heart. We have to get to the Rue Muller and then climb up the steps. I don't suppose the funicular is running so early, and even if it is, I want to go this way. Utrillo painted the steps and the Rue Muller, remember?"

Soon they had left the broad main streets and were in a much narrower one. Some of the shops were opening already and children were playing in the gutters. Drina continued briskly on her way, filled with the nameless excitement that always gripped her when in search of new places. This was Paris on a lovely April morning and somewhere above them lay La Butte de Montmartre that she had longed so much to see.

She found the steps and stopped for a long moment to stare about her: at the little street behind, at the steps rising so steeply above, with just a dead white glimpse of the Basilica of the Sacré-Coeur against the clear blue sky.

Up and up they went and then, looking back, they could begin to see the grey-black roofs of Paris outspread, with, close below them, the great box-like buildings in grey-white and fawn and dull pinks that Utrillo had painted so often.

Glancing at Drina's absorbed face Rose fell silent, not wishing to break the spell. Without speaking again they reached the top and went round to the front of the Sacré-Coeur, where the white steps gleamed in the light and Paris lay now almost completely outspread, a little misty so that they could only dimly pick out the towers of Notre Dame and the far dome of the Panthéon.

"It's wonderful, but it isn't what we've come to see," said Drina, and in silence again they turned and she led the way round the Sacré-Coeur and through one or two side streets, still almost asleep in the morning sun, until at last they stood in a little shabby square, where the trees were in bright green leaf and the gentle angles of roofs and gables, the soft greens and browns and greys, already seemed familiar.

"The Place du Tertre," Drina said softly. "Oh, Rose, are we really here? We've looked at the picture so often in the Tate Gallery."

The little square was quiet still, though tables and umbrellas under the trees spoke of more people later. The only sounds were the twittering of birds and the laughter and quick voices of a few children, who took not the least notice of the two girls.

"It's beautiful," said Rose at last. "Shabby and old and – and remote-seeming. The picture – it was painted looking that way, wasn't it? But the trees were bare and there weren't any tables."

"All the same, it's just as I imagined it. I shall come here often. I know I shall," said Drina.

"I'm starving! Could we get breakfast here?"

"Oh, not yet. We'll find somewhere later." Drina led the way down the Rue Norvins, walking softly over the old cobbles in her rubber-soled sandals, and for an enchanted half-hour they explored the quiet, narrow streets and the little squares, finding again and again something that was already familiar because of their love for the French painters.

They found the Moulin de la Galette and the square that had once been called the Place Ravignon, and Drina's beauty-loving eyes were delighted again and again by the angles of roofs and gables, by the grey-white walls and the peeling paint and plaster, and the sudden, always breathtaking glimpses of the Sacré-Coeur up the narrow streets and alleyways.

"In a way it's a hideous building," she said. "Those white things are more like bottles than domes, but Utrillo must have liked it. Of course it was new when he was painting it at first. I can't imagine Montmartre without it."

Rose was enchanted, too, but she could not quite forget her hunger, and finally they found an open café and Drina, with great assurance but in rather slow French, ordered coffee and rolls for them both.

They ate and drank in utter contentment, and Drina said dreamily:

"There couldn't have been a nicer introduction to Paris. But soon we'll be at work. The first performance is on Monday. Oh, Rose, just at this moment I think we're the luckiest girls in the world!"

3

Out with Igor

That was a momentous day. Miss Whiteway took them to the theatre – in a taxi, not by Métro – and for several hours Drina forgot everything but the ballet, *Casse Noisette*. But by late afternoon they were free and, as they were about to leave the theatre, Igor came up, smiling.

"Would you now like me to show you Paris?"

"Very nice of you," Drina said coolly. "But we'll be able to discover it for ourselves, thank you."

Igor raised his dark, well-marked eyebrows. He had spent a good part of his life in Paris and regarded himself almost as a Frenchman. He adored the city and had only accepted the rôle of Franz because he had doubted whether he would get there otherwise.

"Hoity-toity, Miss Drina Adams!"

"We had breakfast this morning up in Montmartre."

"You don't waste much time. I suppose you had enough money with you?"

Drina, to her annoyance, flushed brightly. The remark was meant as a dig because she had once found herself without money in Milan and had been rescued by Igor. That had been in the days when she scarcely knew him and he had taken her for a child.

"Plenty, thank you, Igor. We brought French francs

with us, as well as Travellers Cheques."

"I could always take Rose," he countered, looking speculatively at Rose's pretty, ruffled hair and happy face.

"I'm going with Drina," Rose said bluntly.

"But I don't understand. What have I done to be so unpopular? Here am I ready and willing –"

"Why don't you take your Cousin Marie out?" Drina asked.

Igor was very intelligent in some ways, but he was not sensitive and he had never even realised that he had deserted the two girls in Edinburgh in favour of his smart French cousin. So he said casually:

"Marie is not here. She has gone with her mother to the Riviera."

"I expect you'll miss her very much."

"Marie knows Paris," said Igor. 'Naturally, as it's her home. But I should have much pleasure in showing it to you. So come and don't argue."

He led them along the Quai du Louvre and the Quai des Tuileries, and into the great Place de la Concorde, where the fountains were playing and the Eiffel Tower seemed very near. Every step of the way there was something interesting to look at, and Drina kept a firm hand on Rose's arm, because there was such a good chance of losing her friend.

They crossed the Place de la Concorde, with Rose squeaking with terror at the apparently uncontrolled traffic, and gained the trees and broad pavements of the Champs-Elysées. And this truly was an enchanted thoroughfare on that warm afternoon in late April, with the chestnuts just bursting into flower. The great avenue stretched away to the Rond Point and to the Arc de Triomphe beyond.

"But I'm so thirsty!" said Rose.

So Igor led them to tables under the trees, near a cool fountain, and ordered tea and cakes.

"This afternoon you are my guests, so there'll be no need for your French francs."

And Drina gave in with a good grace, because it was so lovely to be there in Paris, under the flowering chestnuts, and to know that they would be there for more than a fortnight. They watched the people and breathed the sweet scents of grass and trees and flowers, and the sound of the traffic was only a dull distant roar.

She was happy, but suddenly she was visited by one of those painful fits of nostalgia. It was so beautiful, so colourful, but people spoke truly when they said that Paris was a place for love. In that moment she longed for Grant as she had scarcely ever done before. To explore Paris with Grant ... to walk under the trees ... perhaps to go to Versailles and walk in the spring woods ... to look down on the city from the top of the Eiffel Tower, as they had looked at New York at night from the RCA Building.

But it was a hopeless dream and it was no use dwelling on it. She had Rose, who was a delightful, intelligent companion and, of course, there was Igor. She looked across at his handsome face and knew herself ungrateful. Many a girl might have been glad and proud to be taken about by him.

So she stifled her feelings and did her best to be cheerful and amusing, and Igor swaggered about, airing his naturally excellent French and apparently thoroughly enjoying being out with two attractive girls.

That evening Drina sat up in bed and wrote to Ilonka.

It's so lovely to be here, Ilonka. Rose is thrilled, too: perhaps more than I am. But I really do love it and find it exciting. I think it's one of the places where I would like to live, if it can't be New York.

The rehearsal went off very well. The theatre is quite a big one, very elegant and plushy. It's fun to be Little Clara again, but I am rather scared by the thought of the French audiences. How awful if they don't like us! Though I believe that the Dominick has always had a success here. Of course I won't be dancing every evening, for there are two other programmes – The Lonely Princess, which Paris has already seen once, last year, and an evening of five short Igor Dominick ballets.

After the rehearsal young Igor (only he looks terribly grown up) took us out. Wouldn't take no for an answer. He was really very nice and he showed us a lot of places and buildings, though he thoroughly despises tourists and touristy places. He really does know Paris and he really does love it, so it was quite enlightening to see it with him.

He took us on the Métro back to the Place de la Concorde and I think I can manage it now. It's quite easy once you've had a good look at a map and realised that you have to know the destination of each line.

We walked up the Rue Royale then, towards La Madeleine, and then along the Boulevard des Capucines to L'Opéra, and I nearly got run over because I was thrilled to see it at last. Covent Garden is impressive when you get a chance to look at it, only it's hard to get far enough away, but you can see the Paris Opera House properly and it's enormous, and so impressive with a sort of stone arcade all along the front high up. Igor says it's far more splendid inside than C.G., but then he thinks everything Parisian better than London. There is opera on at the moment, but there will be ballet most nights next week and the week after. I shall just have to go, even though Miss Whiteway is rather too keen on early bed, and she says that the ballet wouldn't be over till nearly midnight, as it starts late.

Oh, I wish you could see the chestnut trees, and the

policemen doing a sort of ballet dance as they direct the traffic, waving their batons and whistling ... and the bookstalls along the Seine ... and all the cafés. I suppose one could spend a lifetime getting to know Paris, but I mean to do my best to know it well in two weeks or so.

What a long letter! And I'm suddenly very sleepy. I don't somehow think we'll get up at six tomorrow morning, as we did today. Pray for us (or, rather, me) on Monday evening. I do feel rather scared. But everyone is kind, and Renée Randall is charming. I miss Catherine Colby a lot, and it seems so strange to see Peter Bernoise going about without her, not to mention dancing with R. R. all the time.

Love from

Drina

PS. Rose asks me to say that she can't understand a word anyone says, but she thinks Paris is great.

So the days passed, filled with rehearsals and with short, satisfying excursions. Igor took Drina and Rose out several times, but they also often went together, or with some of the younger members of the *corps de ballet*. Rose was rather friendly with one of the youngest girls in the *corps*, Judith Laurie, who lived near the Conways at Earls Court. Then, of course there was Terza Lorencz. Rose had seemed rather overawed at first to be in her company, and stared when she saw how casually friendly she was towards Drina, but Terza was so natural and unaffected that Rose herself soon regarded her almost as a friend.

"No one would think that she's written a best-selling book and a famous play," she remarked.

"She didn't write the play," Drina pointed out. "Though she was consulted a lot."

"You know what I mean. She seems quite ordinary."

They went to the Place de la Bastille and lingered

there, dreaming about the French Revolution and on another occasion, they went to the Luxembourg Gardens and wandered happily in the hot sun, lingering by the pool in front of the Palace and taking pleasure in watching the playing children.

When they went to the Montmartre Cemetery, they found it an eerie place even on a bright afternoon, with its dark avenues and brooding rows of grey-black tombs and vaults.

"The perfect setting for a murder story!" Rose said, shivering. "I call it a horrible place!"

But Drina was fascinated by the extraordinary monuments and the whole strange atmosphere of the place and could not be torn away.

"It's the most fantastic place I've ever seen. Someone ought to paint it. I suppose they have, really."

"You ought to go to the other cemetery, Père Lachaise," Miss Whiteway said that evening. "Chopin is buried there, and Oscar Wilde, and dozens of other famous people. It's rather like the Montmartre one, but it doesn't lie low and more sun gets in. It has an old and a new part."

Adele Whiteway was amused and impressed by Drina's calm acceptance of the great city and told Marianne Volonaise one day:

"She's a born traveller – a cosmopolitan. She so soon makes a place her own. I suppose she was like this in New York."

"She adored it, didn't she?"

"She seems to have done. She often mentions it. She seems to feel that she must go back there one day."

But Adele Whiteway was puzzled by the shadow she sometimes surprised on Drina's face. Or perhaps it was not a shadow, exactly; more a dreamy withdrawal, as though her thoughts were far away. She looked wistful,

almost sad, at these times, yet at other times she seemed
almost wildly happy.

Then Monday came and with it the first performance
of *Casse Noisette*. Miss Whiteway made both Drina and
Rose rest in the afternoon, and Rose, in particular, was
cross.

"But I shan't *be* dancing, only sitting in the dressing-
room all evening. I honestly don't see why –"

"You'll be up late, anyway, and you've both been so
energetic that you must be tired."

They protested, but they slept, and after an early meal
it was time to go to the theatre. Then came all the usual
excitement of a first night, with the extra thrill that it was
a French theatre and the audience a Paris one.

Drina was shivering with nerves as she waited in the
wings in her old-fashioned pink party dress, and Igor,
wearing Franz's equally old-fashioned costume,
tweaked her hair.

"Cheer up! You'll enjoy it, you know."

Drina twisted away impatiently, smoothing her hair.

"Stop it, Igor! You aren't horrible Brother Franz until
the curtain goes up."

"I always believe in getting into the spirit of my part,"
Igor retorted, grinning.

Then the curtain was up and the ballet had begun and
Drina had no more time for thinking. She *was* Little Clara
at the Christmas party, dancing with the guests and then
doing her own short solo. She was lost in the magic of the
ballet that had always been one of her favourites.

The long ballet went on smoothly. The party ended
and Little Clara came down in her nightgown to find her
broken Nutcracker Doll ... the battle between the
soldiers and the mice took place and the Nutcracker
Prince appeared. Clara was borne off through the Land
of Snow to the wonderful Kingdom of Sweets.

Drina always loved the last act particularly, though in it Little Clara had little to do but sit on her throne, smiling and eager and watching the different dances; including the Waltz of the Flowers and the famous Dance of the Sugar Plum Fairy.

She had little difficulty in looking eager and interested, because she really felt both emotions, and it was with regret that she leaped up as the ballet was ending, mingling with the dancers, a small nightgowned figure with flying black hair.

The curtain came sweeping down, to rise again on the full company, and the applause was long and generous, particularly when Peter Bernoise led Renée Randall forward. Then he held out his hand to Drina, so Little Clara took a call with the two principals, curtseying and smiling.

"Oh, Rose! Rose! I did enjoy it!" Drina cried, bursting into the dressing-room, where Rose sat reading. "Oh, Rose, I'm so *sorry* it's so dull for you!"

"No need. I don't mind. And I shall get my chance to dance."

"They liked it. I'm sure they liked it. But there are always the critics."

"I shan't be able to read *them*, anyway," said Rose. "I shan't even try."

"You can read French."

"Not as well as you, and it's a terrible effort. Oh, well, home to bed!"

And they were borne north in a taxi, though Drina would greatly have preferred the Métro and the French crowds. It had been an exciting evening and she was reluctant to go to bed.

4
A Message At The Stage Door

The next morning Drina surrounded herself with French newspapers, having run out before breakfast to get them, and read bits out to Rose.

"They do like it, on the whole. Listen to this. 'The Igor Dominick Ballet Company from London last night returned to us with a charming revival of the ballet, *Casse Noisette*. This delightful ballet, with entirely new sets and some new choreography for Little Clara, was a great success at the Edinburgh Festival last year and now we see why. Though one ballet-goer could not help feeling deep regret for the loss of that great dancer, Catherine Colby, it must be admitted that Miss Renée Randall gave an elegant and technically very pleasing performance. She does, however, seem to lack Colby's warmth. Little Clara, danced, as in Edinburgh, by Miss Drina Adams, a pupil at the Dominick Ballet School, was altogether delightful to watch. Miss Adams did her short dances well, with assurance and gaiety, and she managed to convey, as few other Little Claras have done, the magic of the fairy tale. I shall long remember her expression as she watched the Dance of the Sugar

Plum Fairy. This ballet is a must, even for the most sophisticated Parisian. Let us, in part, return to childhood for one evening, but if we also take our critical faculties with us we shall not be disappointed, for this is a polished production.' "

"Oh, I say!" Rose cried. "What a nice man."

"I think it's a woman, actually. That's about the best, but there are others. This: 'Peter Bernoise, as the Nutcracker Prince in this Dominick Company's production of *Casse Noisette*, proves once again that he is one of the most virile male dancers in any country. And the delightful Miss Renée Randall adds a sparkling technique to her other charms as the Sugar Plum Fairy. Miss Drina Adams made a very appealing Little Clara and wore her nightgown with as much assurance as a ball-dress. At the same time she displayed a very attractive childishness and really seemed to feel great delight when watching the long *divertissement* in the last act'."

"You'll never finish your breakfast, Drina," said Miss Whiteway. "Your coffee will be cold."

Drina took a gulp of coffee and grimaced.

"It is! But the papers are so exciting. And today we can relax. Where shall we go?"

"I'll take you both to Père Lachaise, if you like. It may seem a strange way to spend a morning, seeing a cemetery, but it really is a fascinating place. And we might go to the Parc des Buttes Chaumont this afternoon."

So Drina did her best to forget about *Casse Noisette* and the French critics and they set off for Père Lachaise. It was the warmest day yet and the strange cemetery really was an intriguing place. A man in charge of one of the gates gave them a plan, but even with its aid they had some difficulty in finding Chopin's tomb. They wandered down avenues of shadow and sunshine, discovering many interesting names, but not at first the one they were looking for. But in the end there it was, and Drina in particular stared at it with awe.

"Fresh flowers on it, too! I wish we'd brought some. I wonder if he knows that people are dancing to his music still, as well as just listening to it?" And she did a few steps of the Prelude from *Les Sylphides* on the narrow path, to the surprise and great interest of a French family.

Drina, who had not noticed them, flushed and hastily walked away, having no idea that Adele Whiteway, too, had been moved by her shadowed face, graceful arms and dancer's body. Adele thought briefly that, if she had enough skill, she would have liked to paint the little scene: the young girl dancing by the tomb of the dead musician.

"But I'm a designer, not a proper artist," she told herself, as they left the old part of the cemetery for the more modern avenues, drowsing in the sun and sweet with the scent of box and warm grass.

That evening, instead of going to watch the programme of short Dominick ballets, they all three went up to the Place du Tertre and dined under the trees as dusk fell, and Drina was filled with warm enchantment, even though it was a little "touristy".

"I do so love eating out of doors, and, after all, it's still nearly as Utrillo painted it in the early morning."

"And in the winter," said Rose, who felt that dining in Montmartre in the spring dusk was the most lovely thing that had ever happened to her.

Afterwards they strolled on the terrace in front of the Sacré-Coeur and saw Paris spread out below under the half-moon, and even at ten o'clock it was warm and still, so that it seemed an utter waste of time to go to bed.

But Miss Whiteway hurried them away in the end, down the shadowy steps to the Rue Muller and towards the Rue de Clignancourt, where they stopped a cruising taxi to take them the short distance to their hotel. Drina was sorry that the lovely day was over. She had been happy, though, deep in her mind, was always the awareness that she was not quite satisfied with the company of Rose and Miss Whiteway.

"I'm mean and ungrateful!" she told herself guiltily, as she undressed. "I *love* Miss Whiteway, but it's not the right kind of love for Paris." And once more she thought of Grant in New York.

Mrs Chester had commissioned Miss Whiteway to buy Drina a new dress in Paris.

"Because she *is* growing a little at last. That emerald green dress we bought in New York is looking a little short and it won't let down. She loves buying clothes in foreign countries."

Drina, of course, felt rather guilty about Rose, but Rose was not really at all of an envious nature and she absolutely refused to miss the shopping expedition.

"Next best to having a new dress is to watch one being bought. No, I'm coming with you. I want to hear the sales girl say: '*Mademoiselle est si jolie! Mademoiselle est si-si chic*'."

"She may think Miss as plain as anything," said Drina, giggling, and they set off in a cheerful group to one of the big shops.

There were so many pretty dresses that choosing was quite a problem, but in the end Drina decided on a delicate white one. As she was already beginning to be suntanned this suited her remarkably well.

"But I do love the red one, and that silvery one."

"I like you in white – in summer, anyway," said Adele Whiteway. "I should definitely have that one."

In the afternoon they were again sent to rest, and this time Drina lay tossing, wide awake, because she would so much sooner have been up in Montmartre, watching the children coming out of the school beneath one of the steep flights of steps, and wandering away in pairs or little groups, or sometimes with their mothers, to their homes in the narrow, cobbled streets.

But Miss Whiteway, easy-going in some ways, meant what she said about resting, and in the end Drina did doze. She awoke ready and eager for the evening, and the ballet seemed to go better than on Monday, but perhaps it was only that she herself felt easier, with the terrible critics apparently pleased and no longer on the look-out for things to say.

Miss Whiteway intended to watch the ballet from the front of the house and had said that she would meet them outside the main entrance afterwards. She had told them to be quick, as she would try to keep a taxi, so Drina hastily flung off her nightgown, pulled on her ordinary dress and wiped the worst of the make-up off her face.

The old stage-door man put his wrinkled, unmistakeably French face out into the passage as they approached.

"Mademoiselle Drina, there was a young man –"

Drina, still under the spell of *Casse Noisette*, stopped and stared at him blankly.

"A young man?" she repeated, but in English.

"But yes. A handsome young American, fair and tall."

Drina's heart gave such a sickening leap that she clutched at the wall. For a moment her ears sang and she was sure that she must be dreaming. She *must* be dreaming! A fair, tall young American ... Oh, somehow her thoughts must have conjured him up. Perhaps old Henri was psychic!

But he was holding something out to her.

"Monsieur left a letter to be given into the hand of Mademoiselle Drina. It is here."

Drina took the envelope and saw the writing. She had seen only one previous example of Grant's writing, but his Christmas card was in her bag at that very moment, and she would have recognised his writing anywhere.

"Come *on*, Drina! What's the matter?" Rose, sorely puzzled, was trying to urge her friend on from behind. "You do look odd. Do you feel sick? Shall I run and find Miss Whiteway?"

"No, I'm all right. I'm coming." Drina thrust the letter into her bag and summoned her wavering thoughts. She even managed to say "Thank you very much!" to Henri in French, before they were outside and faced with some autograph-hunters. She signed her name mechanically on their programmes and escaped as soon as she could.

As luck would have it, Miss Whiteway was with the Company ballet mistress and they were apparently planning to have coffee together when the girls had been returned to their hotel. So Drina could sit in silence, while the adults talked, and she gazed out at Paris under the half-moon in a state of dazed unbelief, not daring yet to be happy.

Grant had left a letter! But why hadn't he waited; come behind to speak to her? But Grant couldn't be in Paris. He had only returned home from Europe in September last year and it was extremely unlikely that he was back already. But he had left a letter. She slipped her hand into her bag and felt its crispness.

Oh, why didn't the taxi hurry and get them back to the hotel? Why were there traffic hold-ups on this night of all nights? Why didn't that idiotic policeman stop talking so excitedly to that cyclist and let the rest of the traffic go?

But at last they were there and she was blinking in the brilliantly lighted entrance hall of the hotel. Miss Whiteway, who had come with them, saw them into the lift.

"Get to bed quickly, girls. I'll only be outside, having coffee. It's late, but the French never seem to mind *how* late. Goodnight!"

In the lift Rose was silent, but when they had said goodnight to the friendly old liftman and were walking along the narrow polished corridors, swinging their keys, she asked:

"What *was* all that, Drina? What young man? Was it a fan leaving you a letter?"

"I think it was – was someone that I know," Drina said with difficulty.

"An American, did he say? Someone you knew –"

"In New York. But I don't understand yet. I don't think he can be here."

"He must be, if he left you a letter," said Rose sensibly. She thought she understood her friend pretty well, but Drina really did look odd. However, Rose was not one for forcing confidences, so she jammed her key in the lock and said a quick goodnight.

Drina fumbled with her own key, but at last she had the door open and the light on. She shut and locked the door, flung down her case and bag, then opened her case and took out her beloved mascot, Hansl. Hansl went everywhere with her, for he had been her mother's own mascot.

"Hansl, I'm afraid to open it!"

But in the end she did and revealed a page of Grant's

clear writing. The letter was headed with the name of a hotel down by the Palais Royal.

Dear Drina, (Grant had written)

You will be surprised to learn that I am in Paris. I have a seat for Casse Noisette *tonight, but I thought it might give you a shock if I walked into your dressing-room unannounced. So I am writing this note.*

I came to Paris on a business trip with my father, and then we went on to Munich. Father is still there, but I thought I would come back to Paris and see you dance. I shall be here for several days, so I guess we may have the chance of seeing something of each other. I don't have the name of your hotel, so will you call me at mine? Either tonight or in the morning.

Yours,

Grant

Drina read this letter over and over again; then she turned out the light and stood at her open window, looking out into the deep, almost dark courtyard. But overhead was the clear, starry sky, though she hardly saw it because her eyes were blurred with tears.

It was a miracle. An astonishing, unbelievable, undreamed-of miracle! Grant was not in faraway New York; he was here, in Paris, only a mile or two away. She could hear his voice again in a few minutes.

He had been there at the theatre; he had seen her as Little Clara. And for a sharp moment of regret she wished that it had been in some other rôle, not as a little girl in a nightgown.

Tonight or in the morning … tonight, of *course*. But she had never used a telephone in France. One didn't need money, but things called *jetons* or something.

She snatched up her bag and key again and, shutting her door softly behind her, went back to the lift, then ignored it and ran down the stairs. The hall porter was friendly and interested in the young dancer. He readily agreed to get her the number of the hotel and even asked for Monsieur Grant Rossiter. Then he handed the receiver to Drina and withdrew, and she stood there breathlessly, shaking a little, still not believing …

"Grant Rossiter here."

Drina gave a little gasp and then pulled herself together.

"Grant, it's Drina!"

"Drina! I guess it's wonderful to hear your voice!"

"It's wonderful to hear *yours*. I had the most terrific surprise when I got your letter."

"Yes, I thought you would have. Are you with your grandparents?"

"No. With a grown-up friend who does designs for the ballet, Miss Whiteway. We're at the Hotel Nord."

"Yeah, I see." He always said "Yeah" like that; it sounded like the German *ja*. "And what are you doing tomorrow? Do you have to rehearse?"

"No. I'm free all tomorrow; not even dancing in the evening."

"That's great. Then why don't we go out somewhere? To Versailles, perhaps? I guess I ought to go there."

"I guess I ought to go there, too," Drina said, with a shaky laugh.

"Then I guess we'll go together," he countered, laughing also. "If this Miss Whiteway will let you go."

"I'll explain. She's very nice. I'll tell her that your folk know my grandparents."

"Well, why don't I call for you at your hotel about ten? Then she can have a look at me and see if I look respectable."

"That would be – marvellous."

"Fine. Fine. Then that's what we'll do. Have you

grown any? You looked about ten on the stage."

"I've grown a bit. I'm fifteen and a half now," Drina said hastily.

"My! That's quite an age. Didn't I tell you that you'd get older?"

"Did you? It seems rather slow. Oh, Grant –"

"See you at ten, then," he said, perhaps a shade quickly. "Wear sensible shoes, so that we can walk plenty."

"I always do. I've walked about a hundred miles already since I came to Paris. Goodnight, Grant."

"Goodnight."

Drina was left holding the receiver, feeling drained. His voice was the same; now she knew that she had never forgotten it. But she could not – *must* not let him guess how much he had been in her thoughts through all the months since that last meeting in New York. He wouldn't want to know. He was just looking her up because … But he had said that he had come back to Paris especially to see her dance. Drina went upstairs again in a happy daze.

At his own hotel, Grant Rossiter, very thoughtfully, went out to a pavement café and ordered coffee, his brow creased in a slight frown. He very much doubted if he had acted wisely in making that excuse to get back to Paris, but it had been an irresistible temptation. And in the end he had given up arguing with himself and, with the ticket for *Casse Noisette* already in his pocket, had flown from Munich.

Not even to himself had he admitted how greatly he had been haunted by the memory of the little dark girl he had met on the *Queen of the Atlantic* and then seen in New York. He had known – how could he help it, when girls had been attracted to him since he was in his early teens? – that Drina liked him. He had hated that parting from her after the trip up the RCA Building, thinking that it might be a year or two, at least, before he saw her again.

But he had never realised how much he wanted to see her again and hear her clear, expressive voice, until he was wandering along a Paris boulevard a week or two before and had seen the advance advertisements of the Dominick Ballet Company's visit. *"Drina Adams as Little Clara."* The words had leaped out at him and, scarcely aware of what he was doing, he had gone straight to the theatre and bought a ticket. But even when he had left for Munich with his father he had not really been sure that he would return.

Well, now he was back in Paris and he had spoken to Drina. They were going, if Miss Whiteway allowed her, to Versailles tomorrow. But Drina was still only fifteen and a half. With some girls that could have been considered quite mature, but Drina was, in many ways, young for her age, they lived more than three thousand miles apart, and it was useless and might well be painful to both of them, to allow that first attraction to grow.

Yet – soberly drinking his black coffee, he could not see that he could have done anything else. That other time had been so short. If he saw more of Drina he might get her out of his system; there was always that chance. But she still cared for him, that much had been clear from her voice, when she was not consciously controlling it.

"Oh, darn it!" thought Grant, and gulped the last of his coffee, paid his bill and went up to bed. "I can't help it. She's a sensible kid. She'll know how to take it. And if she's been haunted, too, it *may* just possibly help to lay the ghost."

And, in spite of his troublesome thoughts, he fell asleep happily at last, thinking of discovering the delights of Versailles with Drina.

5
The Magic of Versailles

Drina slept very little that night, and when she did she dreamed of Grant. But each time she awoke it was not with the dreadful feeling of sadness that had happened so often since her return from America. She was filled with hope and happiness. Never mind anything but the coming day out: and perhaps other days.

When at last it was time to get up she put on her dressing-gown and tapped on Rose's door. Rose tumbled out of bed and let her in.

"Hullo! I was just thinking I ought to get up."

"Rose!" Drina hesitated.

"Um?"

"Would you mind very much if I didn't come out with you and Judith today?"

"Well, if I say no it sounds unfriendly. And I always miss you. Besides, I thought you were looking forward to the boat trip on the Seine?"

"I was. Perhaps another day. I'm going out with Grant – to Versailles, if Miss Whiteway will let me."

"Grant? Is that the American? Did he ask you in his

letter?"

"Grant Rossiter. No, I telephoned him last night. He asked me to, because he didn't know where I was staying."

Rose was bursting with curiosity, but did not like to ask any further questions. Grant had been mentioned – casually, certainly – in Drina's letters from New York. Was Drina attracted to him then? But looking at her friend, so childish in her pyjamas and short dressing gown, she could hardly believe in any deep feelings. Still, plenty of girls younger than Drina fell in love. Rose herself was not entirely immune, as she had discovered, for there was a farmer's son in the Chilterns who attracted her strongly, and she found herself making excuses to go to his farm. That had been one of the hard things about leaving Chalk Green.

"But Igor is coming, too. You know he said it was a touristy thing to do, but he'd better come and point things out to us."

"Igor doesn't need *three* girls."

"No, but it's you he likes."

"What rubbish! Anyway, Monsieur Igor can think again," Drina said airily.

She escaped to wash and dress, and, after much thought, put on a pretty pale green dress that showed up her suntan. It was new, so Grant had not seen it before.

Adele Whiteway was already in the hotel restaurant when the two girls appeared.

"Good morning. How fresh and nice you both look. Why, Drina! Has someone given you a present?" For Drina seemed positively to glow.

"No-o, Miss Whiteway." Drina sat down and gave her order to the smiling waiter. She said, after a minute or two, "Miss Whiteway, on the way to New York we met some people called Rossiter. Granny and Grandfather liked them and they entertained us quite a lot in New York. And now Grant – the son, who's about nineteen – is in Paris. He left a note at the theatre last night and later I telephoned him at his hotel. He's coming here at ten o'clock to see you, and may I *please* go to Versailles with him today?"

Adele Whiteway looked at her thoughtfully and with dawning misgiving. She was quick and she had been much puzzled by Drina's moods during the winter and early spring. But here in Paris she was responsible for the girl, and Mrs Chester was very strict.

"You say your grandmother liked these Rossiters?"

"Oh, yes, honestly. And Grant took me up the RCA Building at night."

"Just the two of you?"

"Yes." Drina was tense and anxious, feeling her precarious happiness about to tumble around her. If Miss Whiteway said that Rose must go, too … Rose was a dear, but she wanted Grant to herself more desperately than she had ever wanted anything.

"Well, I suppose it will be all right. Especially if I'm to meet Grant."

"Oh, *thank* you! Yes, he's coming here. You'll like him. He's very – very sensible. Old for his age. Quite grown up."

"Oh, dear!" thought Adele Whiteway. "In a way that makes it worse. But he must know what he's doing. Perhaps he thinks of her only as a pretty, nice child."

Rose was upstairs washing tights and undies, but Miss Whiteway and Drina were waiting on the seats in a corner of the hotel entrance hall when Grant arrived. Drina's heart gave a great leap when he appeared, but, in a strange way, it did not seem as though so many months had elapsed since her last sight of him. How tall he was and how fair, and he was beautifully suntanned, though it was so early in the year.

She stood up quickly and went to meet him and Grant saw with relief that the child in the nightgown had given place to a young girl wearing lipstick and a very pretty dress.

Afterwards Drina scarcely remembered the next few minutes. She introduced Grant and Miss Whiteway to each other and then stood a little to one side while they talked, not hearing what they said because she was watching Grant and merely listening to the sound of his voice. But evidently it was all right, for presently Miss Whiteway turned to her, smiling.

"Well, I hope you both have a nice day. Versailles ought to be lovely, and there may not be many people as it's so early in the year. Only don't keep her out too late, Grant."

"I won't. And I'll bring her right back here."

Then they were outside the hotel in the sunshine and Grant was saying:

"I waited till I saw you. *How* would you like to go to Versailles? I guess we could hire a car –"

"Oh, but that would be terribly extravagant, and I'd love to go by train. I know what station."

He laughed, looking down at her.

"I guess you know Paris!"

"Oh, I don't. Not really. I never saw it properly until last week. But I read somewhere about the trains."

"Then we'll settle for the train." And he signalled to one of the taxis in front of the Gare du Nord and helped her in.

"Oh, Grant!" said Drina, as they sped along. "I can't really believe it yet. But you look very real."

"Sure I'm real," he said easily.

"And your father – you came on business with him?"

"Well, he was coming to Europe with a colleague, but the colleague took sick and had to be hospitalised, so he let me come. Just at the last minute, you know. We flew across. I was so dead keen on Paris last year that he knew I'd jump at the chance."

When they reached the station, Grant asked for the tickets and led her to the right platform. He spoke French well, Drina noted with pleasure. That was one thing that she had learned about him already.

The train was a small local and there were not many passengers. They sat in a corner of the long coach and watched the buildings of Paris giving way to more scattered houses and to spring trees.

In Versailles it was very hot indeed and they walked slowly through the old town towards the Place d'Armes, the great open space in front of the vast, spreading Palace. The Ministers' Court and the royal pavement were cobbled, but Drina walked lightly and easily in her soft, almost flat shoes, and Grant laughed.

"I guess many a girl would be tottering over here in spiky heels."

"I expect they would. But I like to be comfortable, and Granny hates very high heels. Another thing that they say at the Dominick is that high heels spoil our balance when we're young. Some of the girls get cross."

Drina's tension was gradually lessening in the warmth of Grant's presence. At first she had felt unusually shy, for it is always strange and almost embarrassing to be back with the reality after months of dreaming.

Grant seemed very interested in French history and, as Drina herself found it fascinating, they were both soon absorbed in the marvels of the Palace. They were lucky, for there were few people about, and they bought an illustrated booklet and avoided the guides. How vast and splendid it all was! Drina was particularly fascinated to see the Opera House, with its sculptures and antique marble. Then they saw the Chapel and the great, ornate state apartments, and Grant vowed that he was getting a stiff neck with looking up at so many decorated ceilings.

But it was the Hall of Mirrors that Drina liked best, for they saw it quite alone and so could get the full effect of the shining floor, the huge mirrors and the great windows that looked out westwards over the terrace and the gardens to the Grand Canal and the avenue of trees.

The view from the windows was reflected back from the facing mirrors and Drina was enchanted.

"Look! We get it twice! Oh, isn't it a glorious place? It makes me want to dance." And, unselfconsciously, she did dance a few steps, moving lightly and airily over the shining floor, a green vision from any century, in her simply cut, soft dress.

Grant made no comment, but it was a picture that he was to carry back to America. The young, dark-haired girl in the vast hall, so obviously unaware of the beauty of her spontaneous little dance.

Eventually they left the Palace and wandered in the formal gardens, where it was astonishingly hot for the end of April. But Drina thrived in the heat, and it was Grant who suggested a seat in the shade of a high, closely clipped hedge.

"I guess we want to see plenty more, though. The woods and the Grand and Petit Trianons. But first what about lunch? We can find somewhere in the town near the Palace."

So they found a small restaurant in a narrow side street and there ate omelettes and salad. Grant ordered white wine and then looked doubtfully at his companion.

"A soft drink for you, perhaps? Lemonade?"

"I drink wine, if it's well watered. Miss Whiteway

doesn't mind. I'm not a baby."

He laughed.

"I guess not. I didn't mean to insult you."

They ended up with fruit and black coffee, and all the time they talked hard, making up for the months that had passed. Drina told about the winter at the Dominick and about *The Land of Christmas* at Francaster, and Grant about his work in his father's office, of the skating he had done during the winter, and of the shows he had seen in New York. Everything he said Drina stored up to add to her knowledge of him, but for the time being she had stopped remembering that by next week he would have gone again. They were in France, in the sun, and that was enough.

The whole lovely day was to stay with her for many years to come, for everything helped to build up the feeling of enchantment. After lunch they returned to the Palace, crossed the gardens and slipped into the deep, cool woods, where everywhere seemed a little wild and untended and all the more magical for that. Birds sang, the sunlight sparkled on the broad paths, and every so often they came to deserted stone basins, where water dripped coolly and the blue of bugle showed in the long grass near by.

They met few people and, near one of the deserted fountains, Grant sent commonsense to the winds and said:

"Why don't you dance for me here? I'd like to take a photograph." He had already taken a number of colour photographs, including one of Drina in the gardens. She had not been shy then, but now she flushed.

"Someone might see."

"There isn't a soul about. It's a wonderful place for dancing."

"It's perfect. And Igor did once take a picture of me

dancing by a fountain in Italy. It was on the cover of a ballet magazine.''

"Igor? Not Mr Dominick?''

"His son. I told you he's dancing Franz. Well, you saw him last night. My Italian Granny and I took him to Stresa once and I danced on Isola Bella when I didn't know that he was watching.''

If she could dance for that dark-eyed boy who had danced Little Clara's brother last night she could dance for him. Grant was surprised and amused by the stab of jealousy that shot through him.

But Drina didn't argue any more. She put down her bag and began to dance part of her own ballet, *Twentieth Century Serenade*, and Grant, recognising it, for he had seen it in New York, dropped down on a stone seat and did not attempt to take a photograph for some time. But he did so when she stopped in a graceful attitude, slim, elegant arms raised and the sun on her face.

"Thank you, Drina. It should make a splendid picture.''

"Oh, I do hope so! Will you send me one?''

"I guess so.''

They wandered on, and Drina, feeling the haunted quality of the place, was no longer surprised that anyone should think they had seen a vision of Marie Antoinette and her ladies, as two women had once, long ago, vowed they had. Le Petit Trianon was full of memories of the Queen, but she somehow liked the gardens of Le Grand Trianon best, for by then it was evening. The pale pink pillars glowed in the light and the air was almost unbearably sweet with the smell of early hawthorn. A thin mist lay over the waters of the canal and it seemed a dream place indeed.

It was with reluctance that she agreed that it was time to start back to the station and they walked slowly along the tree-arched road, breathing in the fragrance of the spring evening, both very happy. Grant would have liked to hold her hand, but did not dare to do so. He had vowed to be sensible and to keep their relationship on the level of friendship. Nothing else was possible, but it was a hard decision.

It was a decision that was all the harder because he was well aware that the girl beside him would have liked him to. Well, would it really matter? Would it make their parting harder?

Yes, it would, said commonsense. And it was on those grounds, and not because he thought of Drina as a child, that he did not take the small brown hand swinging so close to him. It seemed to him that Drina had grown very much, mentally if not physically, since their last meeting, but he just had to keep on reminding himself that she was only fifteen and, of course, of those three thousand miles of ocean so soon to be between them again. Anyway, there was her dancing. She should not be distracted from that during the vital training years.

But in the streets of Versailles Drina herself slipped her hand through his arm, and this was well justified because of the evening traffic.

"Ought we to go back at once?" Grant asked, hesitating by an attractive restaurant.

"Perhaps not. It isn't very late, and I'm really hungry."

"Then why don't we have a quick dinner?"

So they ate at a table under a red-and-white umbrella as dusk began to fall. But at last they were at the station and stepping into a fast train for Paris.

"It's been the most perfect lovely day!" Drina said, with a sigh, as the taxi deposited them at her hotel.

"Are you dancing tomorrow?" Grant asked.

"No, it's the Dominick ballets again. I'm only dancing once more this week. I'm free all day."

"Then why don't we do something that we really ought to do?"

"Oh, I'd love to! But what?"

"Can't you guess?"

"Up the Eiffel Tower!" Drina said promptly. "And look down on Paris as we looked at New York,"

"Fine! You've got it. But not in the dark. We'll see more of Paris in daylight. How will it be if I call for you after lunch?"

"Oh, yes – thank you, Grant."

"Goodnight, then."

"Goodnight." And Drina went into the coolness of the hotel, to be met in the hall by Miss Whiteway.

"Oh, there you are, Drina! I was just starting to worry. Did you have a good day?"

"The most perfect day, Miss Whiteway. Versailles was so beautiful. Hardly any people and flowers and – oh, lovely! Please may I go up the Eiffel Tower with Grant tomorrow afternoon?"

"I don't know. I suppose so. I like that young man."

Drina did not say, "Yes, so do I!" as Adele Whiteway half-expected. She just gave a dreamy smile and stepped into the lift. But when they were passing the second floor she asked:

"Where's Rose?"

"Gone to bed. It's nearly ten o'clock. She had a good day, too. But Igor missed you. He came here to call for you both."

"Poor Igor!" said Drina heartlessly. "If he did it's a really good pay-back for Cousin Marie in Edinburgh."

"I didn't know you were vindictive, Drina."

"*Is* that vindictive? Well, he did behave badly. Anyway, I don't care a hoot for Igor."

That at least was clear, thought Adele Whiteway, and was rather relieved. She did not think much of Igor's character, though he would probably turn into a first-rate dancer.

Drina herself spared no further thoughts for Igor. She lay in bed in the darkness, re-living that lovely day at Versailles. It had been the happiest day she had ever spent, even counting the days in New York. She had wanted Grant to hold her hand and he had not done so, but a sure instinct had told her that he had wanted to. Grant liked her, but Grant was old and sensible and he knew that if they held hands there were things they might say that couldn't really be said.

Nothing could ever be said, because of all the circumstances, but now she was resigned. Now she was living for each day, and even the future would be happier because of them.

At last she fell asleep.

6

Goodbye Again

So Paris, from then on, was almost as enchanted a city as New York had been, perhaps, at times, even more so. Drina and Grant did go up the Eiffel Tower and looked down on Paris outspread in the sun, and each day they went somewhere else.

Twice Rose went with them and returned vowing that Grant was the nicest person she had ever met. And once Grant took Drina and Rose and Miss Whiteway out to dinner. Adele Whiteway was charmed and impressed, and understood all the better something of what Drina must be feeling. But she made no attempt to force Drina's confidence and only hoped that when the parting came it would be managed without too much pain.

As well as the outings about Paris and its environs there was, of course, still the ballet, and Drina was so continuously happy that she went to the theatre in glowing spirits and enjoyed every moment, as usual, of each performance. Rose had her first chance to dance, and that time Drina sat in the dressing-room, but she was not bored because she could think about Grant.

Rose had quite a success and was not ignored by the critics, who had noted that there was to be another Little Clara. One or two made it their business to be present and were very nice about Rose's appearance and dancing. Though one did say: 'Miss Rose Conway's performance was charming in every way, but she is certainly not so technically good a dancer as Drina Adams. This is, however, not surprising, as Miss Adams has had far more experience. One looks forward, however, to seeing more of Miss Conway's work in the years to come.''

So Rose was pleased and happy and more in love with Paris every day, and the only one who was disgruntled was Igor, who presently attacked Drina as she stood in the wings before the curtain went up.

"I've scarcely seen you lately, Drina. What's the attraction you find in that big American?"

And Drina turned to him coldly, recognising that it *was* attack, but determined not to allow herself to grow ruffled.

"*What* big American?"

"That Grant Rossiter you've been seeing so much of. I saw you one day in the Tuileries Gardens, though you didn't see me. Oh, but he is a fair giant! Me, I do not like big men."

"He isn't all that big. It's just that you're rather on the short side," said Drina. It really was difficult not to be nasty when Igor took that tone.

And Igor drew himself up, saying, at his most French:

"Height I do not need. I am tall enough for a dancer. And I shall be a great dancer, with all the girls waiting for me at the stage door."

Drina laughed at his conceit, well aware that she had barely pricked it by her treatment of him.

"How you'll love that, Igor."

So the days passed and Drina felt that she really knew Grant. Knowing him only made her like him more, but she was able to regard him more as a friend, for they discovered that they had much in common. For her age Drina had seen many obscure and difficult plays, and had read widely. As well as the theatre, they both enjoyed art and music, and they almost invariably liked the same paintings.

Then came the morning that she had tried not to dread, when Grant arrived to say that his father was flying from Munich that day and they were leaving for the States early the next morning.

She had known that it would inevitably come, and, in fact, it had been deferred for a couple of days, but she could not help catching her breath and saying:

"Oh, Grant!"

But Grant had gone on speaking rather quickly.

"Look! I've got seats for the Opera House tonight. They're doing *La Belle au Bois Dormant*."

"Oh, Grant!" Drina repeated, this time with delight. *"The Sleeping Beauty*! Oh, I have so wanted to go, but Miss Whiteway had always said it's over too late."

"Well, I called her and she gave permission, provided that I deliver you right back here afterwards. And now what shall we do today?"

In the end they visited some of the places they had liked best: the Parc Monceau and the little streets and squares of Montmartre. For Drina had passed on her love of La Butte to Grant. While they were up there Grant bought Drina a number of reproductions of modern paintings of Montmartre scenes and she was delighted with them.

"I'll have them framed and hang them in my room."

The sun shone warmly, as it had done almost every day since she arrived in France, and mostly she was happy, though occasionally she remembered that tomorrow Grant would not be there to share everything with her.

Evening came at last and Drina ran upstairs to dress. Grant was having dinner with his father and calling for Drina afterwards.

While Drina was zipping up her new white dress, Rose came in, carrying her bag and looking very pretty in a pink dress.

"Well, I'm off! Have a nice time!"

"Oh, Rose, where are you going?" Drina asked guiltily. She had been deserting her friend dreadfully, though Rose seemed to bear no malice.

"Out with my boyfriend, ducks," said Rose, very cockney.

"Your *boy*friend?"

"Yes, mate, you ain't the only one. I'm consoling Igor. We're having a meal and going to the cinema."

"Did – Miss Whiteway say anything?"

"Not a thing, except to tell me not to be too late. She knows that my Mum wouldn't mind, because I told her. Mum *expects* me to go out with boys now. She was married on her seventeenth birthday."

"But you don't usually, do you?"

"No, of course I don't. Until now I've been one of Chalk Green's delicate little flowers. But don't forget that I'll be back in Earls Court after this. I may as well get my hand in, you know." And Rose gave a wicked grin,

"You'll be too busy with homework, and they'll make you keep up your music."

"Oh, well, I'll console dear Igor while he wants me to. Though you can console him yourself tomorrow."

"I shan't want to. Oh, Rose, I *am* sorry I've deserted you so. But you do understand?"

"I understand all right," Rose said, suddenly perfectly serious. "But that's not to say I shan't be glad to have you back. You look really nice and I hope you have a lovely last evening."

The last evening! When Rose had gone and she was thoughtfully clipping on little blue ear-rings, Drina sighed. But she *could* not grumble when fate had been so wonderfully kind and she talked cheerfully throughout dinner with Miss Whiteway.

Grant arrived on time, looking handsome in evening dress, and they were whirled away to *l'Opéra* in a taxi. It was wonderful to arrive at the Opera House and to see the splendid main staircase, with its glittering lights and ornate decorations.

Their seats were in the raised block behind the stalls, and, with a contented sigh, Drina sank down and opened her programme.

"I always wanted to come here. And with *you*, Grant –" But she did not finish the sentence.

"It sure is an impressive place, though the actual theatre is smaller than I expected."

"Yes, it is. Nothing like so big as Convent Garden, or the Metropolitan in New York."

Soon afterwards the overture began and then the curtain rose on the christening scene of *The Sleeping Beauty*. Drina settled down to enjoy the ballet and to note the differences between this French production and those she had seen in London.

In the first interval they walked slowly about some of the splendid rooms. One was huge and extremely ornate, like a ballroom, and it was fascinating to watch the people.

"But we never went out on to the balcony!" she cried, as the bell rang.

"I guess we will next time. It will be quite dark by then and we can see the lights."

The ballet was beautifully produced and the ballerina

who was dancing the rôle of Aurora had a superb technique, but, as the long act went on, Drina's attention gradually wandered. How *could* she think even of wonderful dancing when she was with Grant for the last time? Cautiously she turned her head a little to look at him and he seemed absorbed in the ballet, but suddenly his hand moved gently and his fingers lay lightly on top of hers.

Drina sat tensely, almost afraid to breathe in case he thought better of it. Even that light touch was an infinite comfort. But the minutes and even the hours were flying and soon the moment of parting would have to be faced.

It was lovely to walk along the open stone arcade in the warm night air, and to lean side by side over the balustrade, looking down the Avenue de l'Opéra.

"I am here in Paris. I am here with Grant," Drina thought and her heart twisted at the knowledge that, by tomorrow evening, he would be back in New York, while she was dancing in France.

Afterwards she could never remember the rest of the ballet, but the end came, the curtain fell and rose again to enthusiastic applause. Drina clapped with the rest, but her hands felt cold in spite of the warm air.

"It's twenty before twelve," said Grant.

"Oh, Grant, couldn't we walk? It wouldn't take long."

"No, I promised Miss Whiteway. It will have to be a taxi."

There was a tremendous crowd outside and the Place de l'Opéra was jammed with cars. Drina hoped fervently that there would be no empty taxis, but Grant, with his customary efficiency, had soon secured one and was helping her in.

She sat in a corner of the back seat, a little huddled,

not knowing what to say. The journey would be so short. If only there might be a traffic hold-up! If only –

Grant was thinking much the same thing, and admitting to himself at the same time that it would be better to get it over quickly. As they swung into the broad street near Drina's hotel he said:

"It's been great and I shan't forget seeing Paris with you. And don't forget what I told you in New York. I may be in London some time next year and then I shall see you dance again."

"You m-may not. I s-shall still be a student at the Dominick."

"Then you shall take me to Covent Garden. You will, won't you?"

"Of course I will."

"Fine. And what about writing to me occasionally and telling me all the news?"

"Oh, Grant, I'd like to."

"When you have time." The taxi was stopping and Grant spoke to the driver in French, asking him to wait. They both got out and Drina fought hard with herself, trying to be calm and unemotional.

Grant took her firmly into the hotel entrance hall and they said goodbye under the interested eyes of the night porter.

"Goodbye, then. It's been great."

"Goodbye, Grant."

"And now I shall never hear his voice again," she thought, going blindly towards the lift. "Because a year is endless, and he may not even come then."

Alone in her room she dropped her bag on the bed and then knelt on the floor, burying her face in her arms on the coverlet. But she shot upright when there was a light knock at the door.

All she wanted was to be alone, but she had to open

the door. And there was Adele Whiteway in her dark red housecoat. Without speaking she entered, pushed the door to behind her and sat down on the bed.

Drina, who had turned away to fiddle with some pots on the table, said in a muffled voice:

'I'm sorry I was so late."

"Come here, my dear."

Drina hesitated and then spun round and faced her friend. It was useless to disguise the tears and suddenly she didn't want to try. She sat down on the bed beside Miss Whiteway and sniffed into a handkerchief.

"I c-can't help it, but I'm not miserable really. It's just – well, he's gone and it was so lovely. Thank you for letting it happen."

"I only hope I was wise," said Adele Whiteway.

"Oh, you were. It was the way I wanted it. I don't suppose you understand, but if you say – say that I can't be in love at fifteen I'll – I'll –" She knew, because Igor had told her once, that Miss Whiteway had been engaged to a pilot. He had been killed in an accident three days before their marriage. Adele Whiteway had never mentioned this to Drina, but surely it ought to help, even though she must have been quite grown up, years older than fifteen and a half.

Miss Whiteway was saying calmly:

"I won't say it. Why should I? When I was fourteen I was so much in love that I couldn't eat or sleep, and you seem to have been doing both."

"*Were* you? What happened?"

"He went away to another town and forgot all about me. If he ever knew I existed. But I've never forgotten how acutely I suffered, and, as you say, you've had it the way you wanted it. You've been happy, haven't you?"

"Oh, I have! I never knew I could be so happy. But you won't tell Granny?"

"No. But why don't you tell her yourself?"

"I couldn't. I couldn't bear it. Even though she did once say that *she* was in love when she was very young. You can't tell the people who are – are related to you things. I haven't even told Rose, though I think she understands."

And then, before she knew it, the whole story was pouring out in a flood of words. The meeting with Grant on the ship, the realisation that she was in love years before she had expected it to happen, the further meetings in New York and that last evening on the high terrace of the RCA Building. And her feelings afterwards, the way she couldn't forget, the long, vaguely unhappy winter.

"I knew there was something wrong," said Adele Whiteway.

"But now, though I feel awful at the moment, it *won't* be so bad. I know it won't. I shall miss him, perhaps more, but now I understand better and know him better. I shall get on with my work and – and some day he may come again. You see, this is the third time we've said goodbye. Because I thought almost until the moment when I got off the ship that I shouldn't see him again. I didn't know then that the Rossiters had invited us all to their apartment. So this is the third time and now I think perhaps we may meet again. But –" it was a painful cry – "I can't see a future in it. Not really. He'll get a real girlfriend, an older one. And I – even if I were old enough to be engaged, I've got to dance."

"You still feel that?"

"Yes. I do. It *is* the strongest thing. I never meant to marry until I was about thirty –"

"Your mother did."

"Yes, and she married a foreigner. But he did work in London. Oh, Miss Whiteway, isn't life difficult?"

"Very," said Adele Whiteway, as usual not mincing matters. "You've got a problem and you've seen it rather too early. But it will work out and, meanwhile, you're being sensible. You've had your lovely time, and I'm relieved to think that I was right, after all."

"I'll always be grateful to you. I can't honestly say that Granny would have let me go about with him so much. Anyway, she might have guessed how I felt. But in my letters I have told her about Grant being here. I wouldn't keep it all from her."

"No, I shouldn't. Your Granny loves you and wants the best for you. As a matter of fact, I think she'd be glad if you married young instead of dancing, even perhaps if it meant living in America."

"I shan't do that. I may not even have the chance. No, it's over, but with a sort of strong thread holding us."

"Then it isn't over," Adele Whiteway said, with a sigh.

"Oh, well, I don't know. He's going more than three thousand miles away. How I hate that loathsome Atlantic!"

Soon afterwards Adele Whiteway went away and Drina went to bed. But not, at first, to sleep. There was too much to think about.

7

Mr Dominick
Telephones

After that, of course, they only had a few more days in Paris, and Drina, true to her resolution, honestly did her best not to think about the past. She was greatly helped by the fact that she did genuinely love and enjoy Paris.

Everyone but Igor was tactful and she was casually welcomed back by Judith, Terza and the other youngest members of the *corps de ballet*. Igor, of course, could not let the matter rest, which was perhaps understandable.

"So he's gone – that big American. And now we may have our Drina back."

"You may do as you please," Drina retorted. For after Grant, in spite of his assurance and great good looks Igor seemed more than ever a shallow and unsatisfactory companion.

"What a cat you are! And one would never think it, seeing sweet Little Clara sitting on her throne, smiling and clapping."

"Now *you* are quite like Brother Franz," Drina said lightly, and suddenly they both laughed.

"It's a rotten part," Igor said. "I shall see that they

give me a better one next time."

"There may not be a next time for ages. Soon we'll be back at the Dominick, working like anything."

"But don't forget that next year I shall be a Senior student. In September, that is."

"I had forgotten. There's no chance that *you* won't be accepted."

"Not when I'm Igor Dominick's son and such a wonderful dancer already," Igor said solemnly and she made a movement as though to hit him.

Igor ducked and laughed. If he could not get her notice any other way he enjoyed annoying her.

On their last afternoon in Paris Drina and Rose went up to Montmartre and wandered along their favourite little cobbled streets.

"I have loved it so," Rose said sadly. "I don't want to go home. For one thing it means getting used to the Dominick again, and we've missed a few days of term."

"You'll be all right, Rose. And Christine has gone."

"Yes, but I've been at Chalk Green for two years. That's a long time. *You* had quite a struggle when you went back after less than a year in the Chilterns."

"I know I did, but I didn't have you. Now we'll be together. Only you do understand that I can't desert Ilonka? I like her and I can't hurt her feelings."

"Oh, of course. We'll make a threesome. Ilonka's really nice. It will be good, in lots of ways, to get back to Red Lion Square, but I shall miss the country and I *wish* we had a larger house."

"It is difficult."

"Difficult! I'll say it is. It's given me 'ideas'. There's no denying that, I'm afraid."

"But you wouldn't have missed it?"

"No, I would not. And in a few months, no doubt, I

shall be an out-and-out Londoner again. I love summer in London. We'll do all sorts of things."

"Yes, we'll go to Covent Garden, and sail up and down the Thames, and to open-air plays in Regent's Park. All sorts of things. And perhaps you can stay with me sometimes at weekends, if your mother wouldn't mind."

"Oh, Mum doesn't fuss or try to make us do things her way. She's the best mother anyone ever had." Rose's tone was absolutely sure, but in her heart she was even more uneasy than she had said about the coming changes. Chalk Green *had* given her ideas – of space and luxury, travel and material possessions. But she was a sensible girl, and basically down to earth, and Drina, understanding very well, was sure that her friend would soon settle down to the different way of life.

So, that evening, they had an early meal and went to the theatre down by the Seine for the last time, and for the last time, too, Drina got made-up and put on her old-fashioned pink party dress.

Dancing in *Casse Noisette* had been the greatest fun, after that first rather frightening performance, with the critics in the audience, and, as usual, she was truly sorry that it was over.

For the last time she watched the *divertissement* in the last act and then rose to weave in and out of the dancers before the curtain fell. When they had taken their last call Peter Bernoise, still holding her hand, looked down at her.

"Goodbye, Little Clara. I believe you go home tomorrow?"

"Yes, early in the morning. Goodbye. Give my love to Miss Colby." But perhaps it was silly to call her that now, when she was just Mrs Peter Bernoise.

"I will. She's always very interested in your progress. What are your next plans?"

"Work," said Drina, so grimly that he laughed.

"The same goes for all of us. We've got a big new production coming along."

Outside the theatre there was the usual crowd of autograph hunters, all chattering in excited French, and Drina signed her name a couple of dozen times and then was whisked away with Rose in a taxi.

The next morning they went across to the Gare du Nord and took their reserved seats on the train, and, as they moved slowly out of Paris, Drina looked up for the last time to the Sacré-Coeur on its hill.

"Dear Paris and *dear* Montmartre! How I hate going away from places."

But it was not so bad as sailing away from New York, because Paris really was quite near, and, as Ilonka had once said, she could come back one day.

Mrs Chester was at Victoria to meet them, and Mr Chester was outside in the car. Rose was put into a taxi, and then the Chesters ran Miss Whiteway home.

"Drina looks very well," said Mrs Chester, studying her granddaughter closely.

"Oh, I think she is. She loved Paris."

"I hope that she and Rose were no trouble?"

"No trouble at all," said Adele Whiteway gravely. "It was a pleasure to have them with me."

Drina had scarcely been home for half an hour when the telephone rang and Mr Chester called to her:

"Mr Dominick wants to speak to you, Drina."

"Mr *Dominick*?" Mr Dominick had not stayed in Paris with the Company, but had returned to London after the first day or two.

"You seem greatly honoured," said Mr Chester gravely.

Drina went doubtfully to the telephone and heard the Director of the Company's decisive voice.

"Drina? How are you, my dear? Enjoy Paris?"

"Every moment, thank you. It was wonderful!"

"Well, I'm afraid you've come back to more work."

"Oh, I know. Back to school on Monday." But he couldn't have telephoned to say that.

"I'm not so sure Well, you'll manage to fit in a few hours of school, no doubt, but it looks like being a special rehearsal at the Queen Elizabeth Theatre at ten on Monday."

"But –"

"They've been on to me, and I'm afraid I've more or less arranged it for you. I remembered what you said about being in *Diary of a Dancer*. Giovanna has to have at least three weeks' rest, you see. The play's run for several months and apparently she is feeling the strain. She had a few bad colds and is run down. Then the understudy is leaving, by arrangement. She's got a part in a touring company. So they'll have to rehearse another understudy, and they want *you* to take over the part of the little sister as soon as possible."

"Oh, Mr Dominick! I always felt I should have done it."

"Well, now's your chance for a few weeks. Shall I tell them you'll be there on Monday?"

"Oh – yes, of course. I couldn't refuse."

Drina left the telephone feeling rather dazed. She was tired and had scarcely had time to savour being at home. She had not even unpacked.

"Granny! Grandfather! I'm to take Giovanna's place in *Diary of a Dancer* while she has a rest."

"Oh, really!" exclaimed Mrs Chester, annoyed. "It's too bad of Mr Dominick. It'll be too much for you, with school as well."

"I guess I'll manage. I've *got* to do it."

"You 'guess'! Is that Grant's influence? What was he doing in Paris?"

"On business with his father," Drina said casually and went to her room, where she opened her largest case and found the prints that Grant had bought her. She stood hugging them against her chest, remembering.

But then her thoughts went to the immediate future.

If she acted in *Diary of a Dancer* for a few weeks one thing, at least, would be settled. She might get rid of her feeling of guilt. It was something real and difficult to do and she would put her heart into it.

Outside in the passage she heard her grandmother's voice:

"It really is too bad. She never has time to be a child."

"I think she's finished with childhood," said her grandfather's calm voice in reply, and Drina sighed.

It was true. She might still look disconcertingly young, but she *wasn't* a child. And she looked back to the time before New York without regret.

DRINA

Follow Drina's fortunes, from her first ballet lessons to her triumphant appearances on stages throughout the world, in the popular Drina series of books.

Ballet for Drina	£2.99 ☐
Drina's Dancing Year	£2.99 ☐
Drina Dances in Exile	£2.99 ☐
Drina Dances in Italy	£2.99 ☐
Drina Dances Again	£2.99 ☐
Drina Dances in New York	£2.99 ☐
Drina Dances in Paris	£2.99 ☐
Drina Dances in Madeira	£2.99 ☐
Drina Dances in Switzerland	£2.99 ☐
Drina Goes on Tour	£2.99 ☐
Drina, Ballerina	£2.99 ☐

All Simon & Schuster Young Books are available at your local bookshop or can be ordered direct from the publisher. Just tick the titles you want and fill in the form below. Prices and availability subject to change without notice.

Simon & Schuster Cash Sales Department, PO Box 11, Falmouth, Cornwall, TR10 9EN, England.

Please enclose a cheque or postal order to the value of the cover price and allow the following for postage and packing:
UK: 80p for the first book, and 20p for each additional book ordered up to a maximum charge of 2.00.
BFPO: 80p for the first book, and 20p for each addition book.
OVERSEAS & EIRE: £1.50 for the first book, £1.00 for the second book, and 30p for each subsequent book.

Name ....

Address ....

....

Postcode ....